Disclaimer & Copy Rights Notice

This is a work of fiction. The characters, places, and incidents depicted are entirely a product of the author's imagination. Any resemblance to real persons, living or dead, or actual events is purely coincidental and unintended. The author and publisher bear no responsibility for any perceived similarities.

Don't Read Me

Baaghi follows the entwined journeys of two strangers—Zafir, a brilliant mind driven by his obsession with scientific discoveries, and Khadija, a quiet rebellion girl shaped by the shadows of neglect. The story begins in the present, then slips into the echoes of their pasts, revealing two worlds that seem destined never to meet. Yet fate orchestrates their unlikely collision, testing the foundations of pain, trust, and love—until, in a stirring final act, they find a home in each other.

This novel has a chilling and mysterious opening where a military collides with an impossible phenomenon—a missile suspended mid-flight.

Certainly, Baaghi is more than a title—it's a testament. A declaration that not every rebellion is defiance, and not every fighter picks up arms. Some fight with silence. Some with survival. And some—like Khadija and Zafir—fight by standing still until the truth circles back and kneels.

The novel's heartbeat isn't just justice—it's transformation. We see how trauma need not harden people into vengeance; instead, it can shape them into vessels of grace. The most powerful revolution in Baaghi is not loud. It's when Khadija walks away from wealth with her head high. When Zafir chooses purpose over recognition. And when silence between two hearts finally gives way to understanding and love. Sound's too intricate! Well , I told you already 'Don't Read Me', if you are still reading, it is not my fault.

Prologue

In an era where countless stories emerge each day, this novel was not written merely to add to the volume—but to speak to the heart. Across numerous novels, the author has consistently sought to weave emotional and societal threads into narratives that explore justice, love, resilience, and the enduring strength of human connection.

Originally penned in Urdu, these works reflect the rhythms and realities of South Asian life, interwoven with the nuanced experiences of those who navigate the complexities of migration and cultural duality. Their rendering into English marks not just a linguistic shift, but a heartfelt effort to open these stories to a broader audience—inviting understanding across cultures and continents.

Readers from the subcontinent may find echoes of their own lives within these pages, while those in the West are welcomed into a rich tapestry of Eastern traditions, spiritual values, and universal human experiences that transcend borders. I hope these stories spark empathy, reflection, and perhaps even healing—wherever in the world they are read.

Zafir – ظافر

An Arabic masculine name meaning "victorious," "triumphant," or "one who prevails."

Khadija – خدیجہ

A revered Arabic feminine name meaning "born ahead of time," or "trustworthy," or "respect."

Baaghi – باغی

Baaghi is an Urdu word that translates to "Rebel," or "One who defies authority or injustice.

Author's Note

In an era where countless stories emerge each day, this novel was not written merely to add to the volume—but to speak to the heart. Across numerous novels, the author has consistently sought to weave emotional and societal threads into narratives that explore justice, love, resilience, and the enduring strength of human connection.

Originally penned in Urdu, these works reflect the rhythms and realities of South Asian life, interwoven with the nuanced experiences of those who navigate the complexities of migration and cultural duality. Their rendering into English marks not just a linguistic shift, but a heartfelt effort to open these stories to a broader audience—inviting understanding across cultures and continents.

Readers from the subcontinent may find echoes of their own lives within these pages, while those in the West are welcomed into a rich tapestry of Eastern traditions, spiritual values, and universal human experiences that transcend borders. I hope these stories spark empathy, reflection, and perhaps even healing—wherever in the world they are read.

Scene 1

The Suspended Sky

"The intel checks out—it's been verified multiple times. That's precisely what occurred."

The senior official shook his head, incredulous. "Are you telling me we launched the missile, it took flight as expected, but the moment it crossed into hostile airspace... it just froze mid-air? And they took out all four missiles before they could strike?"

The commanding officer's voice carried the weight of unease. "No one expected this. Even strategist in the capital reviewed the footage—he says it's beyond current technological explanation. Our systems are known for their reliability and accuracy. But this phenomenon... it wasn't hidden. Hundreds witnessed it."

"This is unprecedented. Get in touch with the Air Force leadership immediately. And relay this to the head of government without delay," the official instructed, visibly shaken.

Scene 2

Echoes Under the Northern Lights

Fifteen Years Ago — Canada

"Sweetheart, it's quite late now. Come on, time to stop working and get to bed."

"Just a little longer, Mummy. I'll sleep soon."

Zafir replied without looking up. He was perched in a corner of the annex, hunched over his telescope, eyes locked on the sky like it held secrets only he could decipher.

At thirteen, he was still in school, but his obsession with science—particularly astrophysics—ran deeper than most could understand. He had begged his parents to clear out the small annex they once rented to tenants, and turned it into his tiny lab, his sanctuary. While his two younger brothers and sister showed no interest in his experiments, Zafir found comfort in the solitude of discovery.

His family lived in Iqaluit, the capital of Nunavut in Northern Canada. His father held a job with the city government. Years ago, they'd emigrated from Pakistan, initially settling in Winnipeg, Manitoba. But as the economy worsened and jobs grew scarce, they were eventually forced to seek work in more remote areas—and so they arrived in Iqaluit.

Nunavut, nestled in Arctic Canada, was vast, wild, and sparsely populated. Snow-covered mountains, dense forests, and countless icy islands stretched far beyond the horizon. The territory's remote capital had no road access; travel was limited to air or sea. The indigenous Inuit were known for their vibrant artwork, intricate carvings, and hand-sewn clothing. Among Iqaluit's population of 7,500, a few hundred Muslims had formed a small but steadfast community, establishing a modest mosque under the Islamic Society of Nunavut.

From the doorway, his mother called again,

"That's enough, sweetheart—please come inside. Your daddy's already asked about you twice."

"Alright, Mummy. You go ahead, I'll clean up and be in in two minutes," Zafir replied.

When his mother stepped inside, her husband glanced up with mild frustration.

"This interest of his is bordering on obsession now. He needs a serious talk. That little 'temple of science' of his is becoming an unhealthy fixation."

She sat down and sighed, "He'll grow out of it. Besides, he's never neglected school—his grades are the best in the class."

Still worried, Zafir's father muttered,

"Even so, all this time he spends on pointless experiments is bound to catch up with him. Instead, he should help out—tutor his younger siblings or lend a hand around the house. At the very least, he could wake up early and clear the snow from the driveway."

His wife gave him a gentle smile.

"Don't worry. I'll sit down with him tomorrow and talk it through."

Scene 3

Fractures in the House of Silence

Fifteen Years Ago — Sharjah

"Marrying you brought me nothing but sorrow and suffering. You've ruined my life!"

Ramzan shouted at his wife Arifah, his voice seething with fury.

These were not new words to her. Ramzan often spiralled into tirades of blame and accusations. Sometimes it was a trivial issue, sometimes just his own simmering discontent.

Arifah lived in Sharjah with her husband and their six-year-old daughter, Khadija. Ramzan was a 50% partner in a car showroom and its adjoining workshop. They had no shortage of money, but peace was something money hadn't bought. Khadija had grown old enough to notice the frequent yelling, the relentless tension. She went to a school run under the oversight of the Pakistani embassy, but her studies, upbringing, and emotional well-being were crumbling under the pressure of daily conflict.

Softly, Arifah said, "I didn't invite Sarmad Bhai. He's your cousin—was I supposed to throw him out? If he'd shown up when you weren't home, I might have avoided it. But he came to see you. You were there."

"Then why didn't you just tell him I wasn't home? You know I don't want to see him!"

Ramzan's anger didn't waver.

Still trying to defuse the moment, Arifah answered gently,

"Khadija was standing right beside me when I opened the gate. Was I supposed to lie in front of her? She's already shrinking under the weight of this constant tension at home. Should I also teach her that lying is acceptable?"

Ramzan snapped, "You never take my word seriously! You always do whatever you please!"

Clutching her head in frustration, Arifah murmured, "I don't know what to do anymore to make you happy… I just want an end to this daily misery."

"Ah, now you're being honest! You just want to be free of me. Don't worry—that day will come soon enough," Ramzan roared.

"Oh my God! When did I ever say that? I just meant I'm tired of these endless fights, your constant suspicion. I don't want this poison in our home—it's affecting Khadija terribly. I don't want her growing up with resentment in her heart toward you," Arifah replied, her voice heavy with despair.

"Oh, I know exactly how much you 'care' about me. You play innocent, but all this is so you can…"

Before he could finish, Arifah raised her voice,

"That's enough! Don't you dare sling your vile, baseless accusations at me again. Allah knows my heart and intentions are clean—I won't let you drag my character through the mud."

"Yes, of course—how pure you are!" Ramzan bellowed sarcastically.

Meanwhile, tucked under the bed in the other room, Khadija sat frozen, listening to every word. The shadows under her bed couldn't shield her from the storm erupting outside.

Scene 4

The Whispering Skies

"Bhai jaan, what are you looking at in the sky?"

Nine-year-old Saira had wandered into the annex where Zafir was immersed in his work. It was the weekend, and with no school the next day, she had found her way to her brother's little lab.

Lowering his gaze from the telescope, Zafir smiled and replied,

"There's a star I've been observing for several nights now. I'm trying to calculate its position and trajectory."

Saira, nestled between her two younger brothers and her older brother Zafir, couldn't quite grasp what he meant. She just stared at him in wide-eyed silence. Zafir chuckled gently.

"Gudiya, you won't really understand it just yet. Why don't you run along and play inside?"

Saira, innocent and persistent, said,

"Okay... but at least show me what stars look like. How do they appear through a telescope?"

Zafir guided her to the eyepiece.

"Here, look. You'll see thousands of stars scattered across the sky. And tonight, they say we might even witness the Northern Lights."

Saira, peering into the telescope, asked curiously,

"Bhai jaan, what are Northern Lights?"

Brimming with excitement, Zafir launched into an explanation,

"The scientific name is Aurora Borealis. It's a stunning natural light show in the sky—like a curtain of brilliant colours dancing above the earth. You can only witness it in the far northern latitudes—places like Alaska, Sweden, Finland, Russia, and our part of Northern Canada. We're lucky—there are spots nearby where it appears. What you see is caused by electrically charged particles from the sun crashing into Earth's upper atmosphere at incredible speeds."

Saira pulled away from the lens and looked at him, wide-eyed.

"That must look amazing. I want to see it too."

Zafir leaned in conspiratorially.

"It's predicted to appear between two and three a.m. tonight. There's a lake nearby, surrounded by hills—it's a perfect spot. I'll cycle there alone and take plenty of pictures with my camera... but you mustn't tell anyone I went. Alright?"

With a sparkle in her eye, Saira beamed,

"Wow! Okay, Bhai jaan, I won't tell. Pinky promise!"

Scene 5

A Silent Cry

"Amma Jaan, I'm reaching the end of my strength... My patience is fraying," Arifah whispered through tearful eyes. "Ramzan is consumed by his own paranoia and groundless rage. He has no idea how deeply this is damaging our daughter. Khadija has grown so quiet, so withdrawn—she's constantly frightened now."

Her mother sighed, troubled. "I just don't understand what's wrong with him. His three brothers live in Pakistan with their families—happy, stable... Why is he like this? Beta, I know it's hard, but be patient. Try speaking to him with love and wisdom. Don't confront him over everything."

Arifah's voice trembled. "It's not about me, Amma Jaan. I'm trying—I really am. But it's Khadija I worry about. All this constant fighting is affecting her deeply. Just yesterday, I scolded her mildly over a poor grade... and she broke into tears, trembling in fear. I held her and comforted her, but she was so scared."

Her mother's tone softened. "She's just a child, and fear has taken root in her. Handle her gently—she'll understand in time."

Arifah nodded. "I always try... but lately, Ramzan has started keeping his distance from her. And when he does speak, it's to scold her harshly."

"What? But why?" her mother asked, eyes widening in shock.

Arifah hesitated, then admitted with shame, "I don't even know how to say this... but his suspicions have gotten so out of control, he's started doubting... that Khadija is even his daughter."

"Oh my God! Has he lost his mind? How can he throw such vile accusations at you—at his own child?" her mother gasped.

Arifah's voice was heavy with sorrow. "That's what I've been trying to tell you. One day he pushed me so far, humiliated me so deeply, that in a moment of anger I said, 'Fine, do a DNA test. But remember—once it proves she's our daughter, I will no longer have any reason to stay with a man who doubted my dignity.'"

"Oh ! ... What did he say then?" her mother asked, stunned at how much worse the situation had become.

"What else? He did what he always does—yelled, stormed out of the house. Amma, sometimes I wonder if this is a psychological issue—or maybe something even darker at work."

Her mother's voice was laced with unease. "May Allah protect you both... He'll never agree to see a psychiatrist, but start reciting Surah Baqarah at home daily. I'll keep praying too. May Allah bring peace to his heart and clarity to his mind."

Scene 6

Beneath the Icy Sky

Ten Years Later

A young man stood on a weathered boardwalk that stretched out over the icy waters of a lake. His gaze was locked on the still surface, lost in thought, when a soft hand touched his shoulder from behind.

"What's the matter, bhai jaan? Why are you standing here all alone?"

The young man was Zafir. Seeing his sister, Saira, he smiled warmly.

"When did you arrive from Winnipeg, Gudiya?"

"Just about an hour ago. The flight was delayed because of the weather. When I got home, I found out Shakir and Zakir had gone off to college and wouldn't be back till later. When I asked about you, Mom said she didn't know—but I had a feeling you'd be here."

Zafir chuckled gently. "Alright, enough about me. Tell me—have you settled in well? How's Kashif? You should've brought him along this time."

Kashif, Saira's husband, worked as an accountant in Winnipeg. He was the son of one of their father's oldest and dearest friends. Back when the family lived in Winnipeg, their houses had stood side by side. Saira and Kashif had married just eight months ago. Some people thought she was still too young, but their father had only one reply: she was eighteen, and in a place like Canada—or anywhere, really—timing a daughter's marriage wisely mattered.

Saira smiled and said, "Kashif's gone to Ottawa this weekend. He has a conference on Monday. He asked me to come along, but I wanted to visit all of you—so I came instead."

Zafir smiled faintly. "You made the right choice."

Saira studied his face closely. "Bhai jaan… is something wrong? You seem a little distant… sad, even."

He laughed, but it rang hollow.

"You're still my Gudiya. My sweet little doll. Don't go turning into my Nani Jaan, alright?"

Saira laughed, then tugged him gently. "Come on. Let's go sit on that bench by the lake—the same one we used to sit on as kids."

"Alright, let's go."

They sat in silence, watching the lake. Most of their childhood had unfolded in this place. With few families and even fewer children their age, the siblings had become one another's friends, confidants, entire social world. Whenever Zafir disappeared into his thoughts, it had always been Saira who found him here.

After a pause, she asked again, "You never answered my question."

Zafir looked at her, then turned back to the lake.

"Nunavut Arctic College is the only college in the entire province. There's no university. I've done all I can here, but I want to study further. Dad insists I stay. He's even pulled some strings to get me a job at a local fishing company."

Saira gently encouraged him. "Don't lose heart, bhai jaan. Allah will open a better path for you."

Zafir's tone was low and worn.

"Coming to Nunavut was Dad's compulsion… but choosing to stay here forever—that's his decision. There are so many more opportunities for study and work in larger cities. But staying here… it makes no sense to me. The climate is so extreme. In summer, the sun stays overhead for twenty-one hours a day. In winter, daylight shrinks to just a few hours. It's surreal."

Saira asked carefully, "But bhai jaan, you used to be so fascinated by these things. You'd teach all of us about the science behind them. You used to say that what we could observe here wasn't possible anywhere else in the world. What's changed? Why do you seem so disheartened now?"

"I'm not bitter. Just... hopeless," he confessed. "I want to study aerospace engineering and astronomical science—to work in research and development. But for that, I need to continue my education and find research opportunities. And those don't exist here in Iqaluit."

Saira offered cautiously, "If you'd like, I could talk to Kashif. Maybe he can help you with a job?"

Zafir smiled faintly. "Gudiya... I already have a job. That's not the issue. I want to study, to grow... to create. But that's not possible here. Still, don't worry about me. I've come to terms with it."

She looked at him with concern. "What do you mean—come to terms?"

He answered quietly, "I've set aside my dreams... for the sake of Dad's happiness. No child can ever fully repay their parents for their love and sacrifice. But I can at least surrender my will to theirs—and find peace in Allah's eyes by doing so. Come on now, let's head home. Shakir and Zakir must be back, and Dad will be arriving soon."

Scene 7

The Daughter of No One

For Khadija, the past ten years felt like ten lifetimes. Life had tossed her through such turbulent waves that, at seventeen, she felt as though she'd aged thirty years in a decade.

Ramzan's mental illness, instead of improving, grew more dangerous—his temper turning increasingly cruel, abusive, and volatile. Arifah did all she could: she reached out to both sides of the family, hoping for reconciliation. But when no one could rein in Ramzan's behaviour, and the situation grew unbearable, she was left with no choice—she sought khula and ended the marriage.

Afterward, she secured a job in Sharjah and decided to stay there with Khadija. Her only remaining family in Pakistan was her mother, who lived with Arifah's married brothers. Though they urged her to return, Arifah gently declined. She said to her mother:

"They have families of their own now, Amma. Their lives are full with their responsibilities. But you—you're my mother."

By the time Khadija turned ten, a proposal came Arifah's way. She remarried. A year later, she gave birth to a son. Her new husband, Nasir—a soft-spoken man working at a pharmacy—gradually grew distant from Khadija. Before he could become the kind of stepfather they feared, Arifah sent Khadija to live with her grandmother in Pakistan.

At eleven, Khadija had believed her pain might finally end. She hoped no one would shout at her, hurt her, or make her feel like a mistake. But those dreams crumbled like castles in the sand. Her aunts constantly compared her to their children, criticizing her, belittling her. Her cousins mocked her relentlessly. Only her aging grandmother offered love—but not enough protection.

Whenever Arifah called, Khadija would sob into the receiver, "I want to come back to you. Everyone here hates me. I don't belong here." But Arifah had no options. Nasir refused to bring Khadija into their home—or share in her expenses.

In the beginning, Khadija fought back. But eventually, she grew numb and silent. Her education was stopped. She was burdened with chores. When her grandmother tried to intervene, she was warned, "If you want to keep living here, stay out of it."

Arifah was heartbroken when she learned the truth—but powerless. With a second child and a husband unwilling to accept Khadija, there was nothing she could do.

One day, when Arifah called, Khadija refused to speak. Only after persistent pleading—and her grandmother's urging—did she finally answer. Her voice held no emotion.

Aarifa said: "My child, please forgive me... Even if I wanted to, I couldn't do anything for you. But your mother is not selfish... just helpless and powerless."

Khadija replied in an emotionless tone:

"I've even stopped complaining now... and please, don't call me anymore either."

Years passed. Khadija turned seventeen.

One afternoon, as a cousin jeered,

"How much longer will you sponge off us? You've been freeloading for years. When will you finally leave?"

her younger brother came in,

"Khadija, Dadi's calling you. Someone's here to see you."

Surprised, Khadija followed. It had been years since anyone had visited her. Even Arifah had only returned to Pakistan once—and her husband had only allowed a brief visit.

When she entered the room, an older man sat beside her grandmother.

"Say salam, my dear. This is your chacha—Javed," her grandmother said gently.

Khadija stared at him in silence. The old woman nudged her again,

"Khadija, greet him."

Still, Khadija said nothing.

Javed finally spoke, "Beta... Forgive us. We never reached out before, but I come bearing two pieces of news—one painful, one good."

Khadija's voice rose, sharp with pain,

"Don't call me your daughter. Even my own parents never earned that right."

Javed's tone was heavy. "Your father—our brother Ramzan—has passed away. But you… you are our family. Yonu are our blood."

With cold detachment, Khadija replied, "What father? What family? I know no one but my grandmother. Who are you, and why are you here?"

Her grandmother scolded softly, "That's no way to speak, beta. A parent may die, but the bond remains. You should grieve your father."

Khadija's voice cracked with wounded defiance,

"He birthed me, yes—but made my very existence a curse. And now, when I've lived like an orphan all my life, you expect me to mourn? I was born an orphan. I remain one—even now. I want nothing from anyone."

As she turned to leave, Javed called out,

"Your pain is valid. Your anger is justified. But before you go—please hear one thing."

She paused.

"Don't call me daughter," she said. "I mean nothing to you."

Javed answered gently,

"I came to take you home."

Both Khadija and her grandmother were stunned.

"I have no home with you. Please leave."

"Not as my niece—but as my daughter," Javed said firmly.

Her grandmother was equally shocked—but secretly relieved.

"It's a blessing—even if it's late. He's still family. And an uncle can be a father figure," she said.

"You should listen to him, beta."

Khadija flared up,

"If I've become a burden you can't bear, just say it. I'll go elsewhere—but I won't go with him."

She stormed into her room. Her grandmother turned to Javed,

"You don't need me to explain the reasons behind her bitterness. But I'm glad someone has finally come forward to make things right. I only hope she can learn to trust again. She's been carrying pain and betrayal for far too long."

Javed nodded, "Ramzan is gone now. May Allah forgive him. I won't say more—but he did wrong. And Khadija isn't wrong to feel the way she does. But she's part of our bloodline. Our late brother's child. We won't let her cry anymore. I'll return—with her other uncles as well. She must listen to her family now. We want her to live with dignity and peace. She's still a child… but her wounds run deep. Still, I have hope. One day—she will come with us."

Scene 8

The Weight Beneath the Wings

After Friday prayers, Zafir stepped out of the mosque and was making his way back to work when someone called his name from behind.

Turning around, he saw Imam Hassan al-Muqaddadi—a devout Arab by descent and well-respected manager of the local grocery store. Known throughout the tight-knit Muslim community of Iqaluit for his religious knowledge and integrity, Imam Hassan often led prayers and Friday sermons voluntarily, offering spiritual guidance to the handful of Muslims in this frozen corner of the world.

Zafir greeted him politely.

"Yes, Imam Sahib—is everything alright?"

Returning the greeting, the Imam said,

"No problem—just something I wanted to speak with you about. I'm heading to the store now, and you must be returning to work. Could you visit me after your shift?"

Perplexed but respectful, Zafir nodded.

"Of course. I'll stop by between five fifteen and five thirty."

That evening, the two sat across from each other in the small office at the back of the grocery store. Imam Hassan began,

"Before I share something with you, let me first recount a story."

Zafir listened quietly. It was the first time the Imam had ever asked to speak with him in private.

"Once, I was in Calgary for a religious event where a scholar from Pakistan shared a powerful incident," the Imam said.

"He spoke of one of Pakistan's renowned muftis who longed to perform Umrah (Pilgrimage). After many prayers and efforts, his journey was finally arranged. But just days before departure, his father—himself a respected scholar—fell gravely ill. So the mufti stayed behind to care for him."

"One day, his father asked, 'Weren't you going for Umrah?' The mufti replied softly, 'My Umrah is here—with you.' His father blessed him. And since then, Allah opened the way for him to visit Makkah and Madinah numerous times and travel the world spreading knowledge."

The Imam paused, allowing the words to settle.

Zafir sat silently, piecing together the purpose behind this gentle parable.

Imam Hassan continued,

"You, too, are a Pakistani-Canadian. I told you this story for a reason: when a person sacrifices a cherished dream for the sake of Allah's pleasure—especially to serve their parents—they may be rewarded in the afterlife... but often, Allah blesses them in this world as well."

"Serving one's parents is a divine command, a path to His favour. When that mufti chose his father over his own aspirations, Allah elevated him beyond his imagination."

Now Zafir understood.

The Imam added, "I did speak with your father, though he didn't ask me to say anything. I simply felt moved to share this with you."

Zafir responded with quiet gratitude, "Your words aren't unwelcome, Imam Sahib. I'm thankful."

The Imam leaned forward, eyes kind.

"I've heard you dream of aerospace research. But you chose your father's wishes over your own. I truly believe—In-sha-Allah—you will rise in that very field… and people will stand in awe of your success."

"Ameen," Zafir whispered—though his heart didn't echo the hope. In his mind, he had already surrendered his dream, resigned to climbing the ranks of the local fisheries.

Scene 9

The Threshold of Trust

"I don't want to speak to them. And now you want me to just go with them as if none of it ever happened?" Khadija snapped, her voice laced with fury.

Her grandmother sighed deeply.

"Child, believe me—I don't truly want that either. It strikes me as strange too, that after all these years of silence, they suddenly show concern. But you know better than anyone what life has been like here. Your aunts and cousins grow more bitter and cruel with each passing day... and I, with my failing health, can no longer protect you the way I want to. That breaks my heart more than anything."

Tears welled in Khadija's eyes as she folded into her grandmother's embrace.

"You're the only one in this world I love. The only one I trust. No one else here matters to me—not a single bond means anything. So long as you're with me, I can endure anything. I'll be patient, I'll survive."

Her grandmother held her close, but her voice trembled.

"My child, I live to see you... but I'm reaching the end of my strength. I fear what will become of you when my eyes close for good. If they treat you this way while I'm still breathing, I shudder to imagine what they'll do when I'm gone."

"Don't talk like that," Khadija whispered through her tears.

Wiping her own eyes, her grandmother said gently,

"Death is part of life. Your mother... she's trapped in her own struggles. She cannot care for you the way you deserve."

"Don't even say her name. I have no mother, no father. You're all I've ever had," Khadija declared with wounded defiance.

"No, my dear. Don't say such things," her grandmother urged.

"These are ties of blood—created by Allah. You may choose not to acknowledge them, but they do not cease to exist. Your anger is justified, but forgiveness is beloved to Allah. Let go, if not for them, then for your own peace. Move forward with your life."

Khadija scowled. "You want me to forgive them? Just like that? Pretend none of it happened? That my childhood wasn't spent trembling in fear? That my youth isn't passing under a cloud of humiliation and pain? I can't forget. There's a fire inside me—it eats away at me every single day. A rebellion that screams everyone is a betrayer. Everyone but you."

Her grandmother's voice was firm, yet kind.

"Not everyone is the same. After your father's death, your uncle didn't have to come—but he did. I found it strange too, yes—but he's your blood. An uncle can be a father, you know. You'll be safer, more respected with him than you are here. My health is fading. I need you to think carefully, my love. I want you to decide—soon."

Scene 10

Echoes of a Prayer Fulfilled

Back home from work, Zafir sat hunched over his laptop, focused on his screen. A notification pinged—New Email—and he opened it.

As he read line after line, his face began to glow. A sense of exhilaration overtook him. Finishing the email, he jumped up and shouted, "Bingo!"

He checked the time, picked up his phone, and quickly dialled.

"Good morning, Professor Parker. This is Zafir Suhban from Iqaluit—I just received your email and wanted to follow up."

Professor Parker chuckled, "Good morning from Texas! Actually, in your case, it should be good evening, shouldn't it?"

Zafir beamed. "Yes, sir. It's almost 6 p.m. here. You'd written to contact you directly—so here I am."

"Ah yes, your technical paper," Parker replied. "The one you submitted for review before submitting to an international journal. But tell me—what made you think I'd even consider proofreading it?"

"As I mentioned in my email," Zafir began, "I've never had the chance to attend university. But I've spent years studying, observing, and experimenting on my own. Through my research, I learned that you're a respected name in aerospace science—a department head at a leading university. Even renowned space agency—SANA consults you on various topics. Knowing that, I became your humble admirer. When I wrote this paper, I thought—if it could just pass under your eyes, I'd gain the confidence to submit it officially."

Parker responded, "Normally, I ignore unsolicited drafts—too little time, and frankly, most submissions aren't worth the attention. But your paper on Spatial Anomalies caught my eye. I skimmed it initially, but soon I was drawn in. I couldn't believe someone with no formal education had written this. I read the entire piece—and added a few necessary corrections."

"Thank you, sir!" Zafir exclaimed. "I'll revise it right away."

The professor continued, "If you're interested, I'd be happy to offer you admission and a research scholarship at my university."

Zafir hesitated. "That's incredibly generous, sir... but I can't leave Iqaluit due to personal reasons, so attending a university in person isn't an option for me."

After a pause, Parker offered a second path.

"Then consider enrolling in a virtual undergraduate program through a university that offers online courses. While you study, you can work with me on research projects remotely. There's no need to come to Texas—unless maybe for a few days down the line."

Zafir was stunned. He hadn't even dreamed of such an opportunity.

"Sir, it would be an honour to work under your guidance and learn from you. I'll find an online program right away and begin our collaboration."

"Excellent. I'll also recommend your paper for publication in our university's Science and Technology Journal, and you should still submit it to the international journal as well."

When the call ended, Zafir sat quietly, overwhelmed with joy. And in the soft echo of his thoughts, Imam Hassan's words returned:

"Those who give up something for the sake of Allah... their sacrifice never goes unrewarded. In the hereafter—and sometimes, even in this world."

Scene 11

A Door Opens Gently

A month later, Khadija had finally moved into her uncle Javed's home. Her aunt Yasmin and her two daughters welcomed her with kindness and warmth. Javed's two sons lived in another city, studying engineering at a university while staying in a hostel.

Her taya (eldest uncle) and younger uncle Liaqat, both of whom lived in affluent neighbourhoods nearby, had visited her several times—each time bringing thoughtful gifts.

One day, Khadija stood at her window, gazing up at the sky. Her thoughts swirled with disbelief.

"O destiny," she thought, "after all the trials and humiliation… I never imagined happiness and peace could stand just a few steps away, arms open, waiting for me."

She was lost in reverie when a knock came at her door. It was her uncle Javed.

"May I come in, beti? I need to speak with you," he said gently.

"Yes, bade chacha, please come in," she replied quietly. She called him bade chacha, his younger brother chhote chacha, and their elder brother taya.

Javed entered with affection in his eyes.

"Beti, your taya, chhote chacha, and I have made a decision. It's time for you to continue your studies."

Khadija's eyes lit up. "I always wanted to study, bade chacha, but the circumstances at Nani's place made it impossible."

He nodded gently. "We understand. And we're all sorry we didn't bring you to us sooner. But what's past is past. Tomorrow, your chachi Yasmin will take you to an excellent college nearby to get you enrolled."

Khadija, humbled and grateful, said, "Thank you so much. That would mean the world to me."

Placing a loving hand on her head, he smiled.

"You're not just our niece, Khadija. You're our daughter now. It's our responsibility to see you thrive. Here—these are your admission forms and a few other documents. Just sign where needed, and we'll take care of the rest to avoid any delays."

After she signed the papers, he added, "I'll give these to Yasmin. Tomorrow morning, go with her to submit them, and then you can pick up your course books in the afternoon. Oh, and here—keep this."

He handed her twenty thousand rupees.

Khadija hesitated. He reassured her, "Take it, beti. You'll need it for books and supplies. I've already asked Yasmin to pay the college fees."

Accepting the money, Khadija whispered, "Thank you, bade chacha."

Scene 12

When the Universe Answers

After Zafir's technical paper was published in the international science journal, responses began to pour in—some offering academic scholarships, others extending lucrative job opportunities. Yet he stayed the course, enrolling in an online engineering program on Professor Parker's advice while continuing joint research with him. For the first time, Zafir felt that everything he'd once dreamed of was now within reach—without ever leaving home.

One evening, as he was studying, his phone buzzed. An unknown number appeared on the screen.

"Hello," said a voice, "My name is David Warner. I'm an entrepreneur. I came across your article in the science journal—and I'd like to talk to you about your idea."

Intrigued, Zafir replied, "Thank you for reading and appreciating it. I'm happy to answer any questions."

David asked directly, "Is what you proposed in the paper practically possible?"

Zafir responded, "The concept of spatial anomalies and wormholes has been around for decades. It gained public attention in the '70s and '80s thanks to shows like Star Trek. But even today, no one has ventured into deep space. Despite major advancements in aerospace, we remain limited to satellites—no actual spacecraft capable of true deep-space travel has been built. So, it's hard to confirm whether wormholes, as described in theoretical physics, truly exist. They are believed to emerge where the laws of physics bend, altering the space-time continuum. For instance, if a journey from Point A to Point B normally spans fifty thousand light years, a wormhole—if accessible—could make that same leap instantaneous."

David replied, "I'm no scientist, but even I know wormholes in deep space are still mostly speculation. What intrigued me is your idea—not about distant galaxies, but about generating artificial spatial anomalies here on Earth to simulate wormhole behaviour. That's bold, original… maybe even revolutionary. Whether it's practical—I can't say."

"That's something only experimentation can reveal," Zafir said. "In the paper, I tried to present it as theoretically sound using known models and calculations."

David paused, impressed.

"You're remarkably gifted. I'm amazed you're not a formally certified scientist or engineer. Which brings me to this—a rather exciting offer."

"I'm listening," Zafir said curiously.

"You're doing part-time research with Professor Parker, right? And probably earning, what, fifteen hundred or two thousand dollars a month?"

Zafir nodded, somewhat sheepishly.

David continued,

"I'm offering you a full-time job with my company—at twenty-five thousand dollars a month."

Stunned, Zafir asked, "What would the work involve?"

"Exactly what you want to do. I want us to build a lab prototype based on your idea—to attempt generating a controlled spatial anomaly and replicate a wormhole experimentally. And don't worry about funding. Whatever you need—equipment, personnel, infrastructure—my company will provide."

Zafir was overwhelmed—surprised and elated that his paper had resonated so deeply.

"That's an incredible offer," he said cautiously, "but I'll need time to think it over and take advice."

"Of course," David replied. "Take your time. I'll call you again tomorrow, same time. Goodbye for now."

As Zafir ended the call, his heart brimmed with gratitude. Imam Hassan's words echoed gently in his mind: "When someone gives up a dream for the sake of Allah… Allah never lets that sacrifice go unrewarded."

Scene 13

Whispers Behind the Curtain

After beginning her college studies, Khadija found a strange calm returning to her life. That day, however, college let out early—two classes had been cancelled unexpectedly. While some girls lingered in the library, she chose to return home.

As she stepped inside, she heard quiet but urgent voices from the drawing room. Curious, she paused—there sat her taya, Uncle Javed, and Uncle Liaqat, heads bowed in conversation, unaware of her presence. The room felt heavier than usual. Her taya was speaking.

"This paper has no legal standing whatsoever."

Uncle Javed frowned. "What do you mean? It's signed."

Uncle Liaqat backed the elder brother. "He's right. This could backfire if ever challenged in court. It might actually be used against us rather than protect us."

Javed sighed, his voice tense. "Then I suppose all we can do is wait for the right time."

Her taya reassured them, "Don't stress so much. It's only a matter of six months—a year at most. Can't we just let things be for now?"

Khadija quietly slipped away to her room, her mind buzzing. What were they so entangled in? What document? Why such caution?

Scene 14

Between the Stars and Suspicion

The next day, Zafir called Saira and told her about David's unexpected offer. She responded with excitement and disbelief.

"Wow, bhai jaan! That's a no-brainer! I think you should talk to Mom and Dad about it."

Zafir replied, "You're right—but something about it doesn't sit well with me."

Saira asked, "What's bothering you?"

In a serious and slightly troubled tone, Zafir said,

"I keep wondering—what does this man David really want from this experiment? He's already told me he's just a businessman with no scientific background. Then why is he taking such an unusual interest in this idea... and willing to invest so much money?"

Saira paused, concerned now too.

"You have a point. In this capitalist world, people don't even offer water for free—this kind of lucrative offer really is strange. You should talk it through with Daddy. May Allah keep you safe from harm and always grant you happiness."

Zafir smiled. "And you too, Gudiya. Take care—and give Kashif my regards. Allah Hafiz."

Scene 15

A Flicker Behind the Curtain

After speaking with Saira, Zafir hung up and sat in silence, thoughts swirling. A moment later, he made another call—to Professor Parker. He laid out the entire conversation with David Warner. Parker's response carried a weight Zafir hadn't anticipated.

"I had a feeling this would happen," Parker said in a strange tone, "but I didn't expect it so soon."

"I'm sorry, sir," Zafir replied in confusion. "I don't understand what you mean."

There was a dry, almost brittle chuckle from the professor.

"I'm seventy now, Zafir. I've seen generations rise and fall. The world we live in today is vastly different from the one I grew up in. Back then, both students and teachers cherished learning. Now... well, now this generation is too busy with distractions."

"One of my schoolteachers once told me: 'Cultivate your knowledge so well that even the most cunning thief can't steal it.' I built my entire life on that belief. But now, in my old age... even that faith wavers."

Bewildered, Zafir admitted, "Sir, I'm struggling to follow your point."

Professor Parker's voice dropped into a strange, warning cadence.

"You're a brilliant young man, Zafir. You'll understand soon enough. The world today is teeming with intellectual thieves. And they don't just steal ideas—they do it so subtly, you barely realize what you've lost. That's exactly what someone like David intends to do with you."

"Wait—what do you mean?" Zafir asked, his voice tightening.

"In the corporate world," Parker continued grimly, "any research or invention created under a company's banner belongs entirely to the company—not the individual who made it. The intellectual property and copyrights? They become theirs." The professor responded.

"Oh..." Zafir whispered, his chest tightening with unease.

"If you join David's team and this prototype works—even beyond your wildest hopes—then the company will hold all rights. They'll have the authority to mass-produce, sell, and profit from your creation. And if they decide to remove you from the picture? Legally, you won't have a leg to stand on." The professor cautioned Zafir.

The implications were terrifying.

"Then I'll just refuse the offer," Zafir said, anxious now.

But Parker's concern didn't wane.

"You should refuse—but that's not what truly worries me."

"What does, then?" Zafir asked, heart pounding.

The professor hesitated.

"If your theory works—if such a machine becomes reality—its commercial and military value would be immense. David seems like a greedy opportunist. I think he'll back off if you say no. But others... others may not. And that could become dangerous."

"Others?" Zafir echoed cautiously. "What others?"

Parker's voice lowered.

"We'll talk about that another time. For now, focus on your education. Limit your interactions. And most importantly—don't discuss this research with anyone. At least for the next few months."

Scene 16

The First Ray

"You don't really talk to anyone in class... so I thought I'd come talk to you myself," said one of Khadija's classmates, settling beside her during a free period.

Khadija replied flatly, "I just don't like talking to people much."

Her classmate—Aamna—smiled playfully. "What, did your mom tell you not to?"

Startled, Khadija's tone sharpened. "Excuse me?"

Of course, Aamna had no idea what lay beneath Khadija's guarded silence. Her comment had been nothing more than a light-hearted tease.

"Hey, I was just joking—don't take it the wrong way," Aamna said gently. "My mom's always telling me not to befriend boys, and even with girls, she says not to get too close. Just go to college and study—that kind of thing. So that's where the joke came from."

Khadija sighed and softened a little. "Oh… okay. No worries. I guess I just prefer to keep to myself. Please don't take it personally."

Aamna grinned. "Well, you're talking to me now—so, friends?"

She held out her hand.

Khadija hesitated, then reached out and shook it.

Aamna chattered on: "I live in G-8. My dad runs a garments business, and my mom owns a boutique. I have two older sisters—both married. One lives in Manchester, England, and the other in Montreal, Canada. What about you?"

Khadija replied quietly, "I don't really have a happy story like yours... so maybe let's not go there, okay?"

Aamna nodded with warmth. "That's fine. We can talk about it another time. For now—how about some tea and samosas? It's a free period and I'm starving."

Khadija gave a small nod—and in that moment, something quiet and healing began.

Scene 17

The Shadow That Reaches

Following Professor Parker's advice, Zafir cut all ties. He deleted his email and turned off his old phone, purchasing a new one to avoid further contact. For a few days, life returned to a quiet rhythm. Until one evening, a call came in from an unknown number.

A voice on the other end said coldly, "Don't hang up. Listen carefully."

Startled, Zafir replied, "Who are you?"

The voice gave a soft, eerie chuckle.

"Who I am isn't important. What I want—that's what you need to understand. The sooner you do, the safer you'll be. I think by now, you've figured out that deleting your email and changing your number didn't stop me from finding you."

A chill crept through Zafir's spine. He swallowed hard. "What... do you want from me?"

The man laughed again—this time louder, more menacing.

"Now that was clever. A smart man asks the right question. Yes, you should know what I want—I want that machine. The one from your research paper."

"That was theoretical," Zafir stammered. "It's not something I can just build—it was based on unproven assumptions."

The voice turned cunning. "Don't take me for a fool. I know you'll need experiments, specific tools, funding. And for all that… I'm here."

"Even so," Zafir faltered, "I'm shaken. I can't focus in these conditions—and if I can't focus, I won't be able to experiment properly. Your money would be wasted."

The voice erupted in laughter, sharp and cruel.

"A few million dollars wasted? I wouldn't care. What I would regret… is having to remove you from the picture if you fail."

Zafy froze. His voice quivered. "Are you threatening to… kill me? I—I'll report this to the police."

More laughter. Darker this time.

"The people I work with are the police. The court. The law. Go ahead—try it. But know this: it would end this lovely little 'partnership' we've begun. And if the experiment fails… we'll send you 'upward'—for good."

Scene 18

The Last Thread Snaps

One afternoon, while Khadija was home, her aunt came into the room and gently placed a hand on her shoulder.

“Khadija, you’ll have to be strong for what I’m about to tell you.”

Alarmed, Khadija asked, her voice trembling,

“W-What is it, Chachi? Is… is Nani alright?”

Her aunt pulled her into an embrace and whispered,

“Javed just called. This morning, by Allah’s will… your Nani passed away.”

Khadija’s tears began to fall silently, her world lurching again.

Her aunt said softly, “Start getting ready. Javed is on his way. We’re going to your maternal home.”

After her aunt left, Khadija sat in silence, waiting. The tears didn’t stop. Her grandmother had been her only safe place, her only unwavering love—and now she was gone. The loneliness clawed deeper than ever before.

Moments later, her phone rang. The caller ID read Arifah. She was sobbing.

Khadija asked, without warmth,

“Will you be coming for Nani’s last rites? Will you attend her funeral?”

Arifah’s voice broke, “My sweet girl, I wish I could—but I can’t. Nasir…”

But before she could finish, Khadija cut her off.

"You were helpless then. You're helpless now. And if I die someday, you won't make it then either."

"Don't say that! May Allah protect you from all harm," Arifah cried, "Don't speak like that, my sweet child."

But Khadija's voice held nothing but quiet fury.

"Please don't call me again. You erased me from your life—now let me live mine without you."

Through sobs, Arifah whispered, "You don't understand how much I love you. Your words... they tear my heart apart."

Khadija responded in a flat, detached voice.

"Chachi's calling. I think bade chacha has arrived. I'm going."

Scene 19

In the Eye of the Storm

The next day, unable to focus and wracked with anxiety, Zafir left work early. As he entered the house, his mother looked up in concern.

"You're home early, beta. Is everything alright?"

"Just not feeling well, Mom. I've got a bad headache," he murmured, trying to keep his voice steady.

Reading the tension on his face, she said kindly,

"Go to your room and rest. I'll send Shakir up to massage your head."

"No, Mom—don't bother," Zafir said quickly. "He and Zakir have finals coming up. Let them focus. I'll be fine with some rest."

She gently brushed his head with her hand,

"In-sha-Allah, you'll feel better soon, my dear. Go rest—I'll bring you some Tylenol."

In his room, Zafir lay restless. The voice from the call echoed relentlessly in his mind. That morning, the man had called again at the office; Zafy had hung up, claiming to be in a meeting. But the man had said calmly, "No worries. I'll try again tonight."

Trapped in this spiral of dread, he jumped as his phone rang again. His heart pounded—but this time, it was Saira.

Relieved, he answered.

"Bhai jaan, what's going on? You sound so stressed and frightened," Saira said immediately.

Trying to mask it, he replied, "I'm fine, Gudiya. Don't worry about me."

But Saira wasn't convinced.

"Shakir and Zakir may be younger—but you and I have always been friends first. We've shared everything since childhood. Please tell me—what's troubling you?"

After a pause, Zafir admitted quietly, "This isn't just worry—it's danger."

"Oh God—what do you mean? Please, bhai jaan, tell me everything," she pleaded.

And so he did—every detail.

When he finished, Saira was silent for a moment. Then she said,

"Did you tell Daddy?"

"No. He's always resented my involvement in science. If he finds out about this, he'll be furious."

Saira offered quickly,

"Then you need to go to the police."

"Here in Iqaluit?" Zafir sighed. "Our police force isn't equipped for something like this. I doubt they'd be any help."

Worried, Saira said,

"I'm really scared for you. What if those people find their way to you up there? Please—come to Winnipeg. Take a few days off work. Pause your studies. Just come."

"But for how long can I hide at your place? That's not a real solution," he replied, voice tight with uncertainty.

She tried to reassure him,

"If you disappear from the scene for a while, maybe they'll back off. Maybe they'll give up the chase."

Zafir nodded slowly. "I'll speak to Professor Parker. He's been unwell lately, so I haven't been able to reach him. But I'll try again."

Scene 20

A Ride Toward Something New

Two weeks later, a half-day at college meant students were headed home earlier than usual. As Khadija approached the usual pickup spot and took her seat in the van, the driver turned to her apologetically.

"Ma'am, the van's having mechanical issues. I've called the company—they're sending another vehicle. But it might take a while."

Khadija stepped aside. Just then, a car pulled up nearby. The rear window lowered—it was Aamna in the back seat.

"I was just leaving when I saw you standing here. What's going on? Is there an issue with the van?"

"Yeah," Khadija replied, "The van broke down. The driver's called for a replacement."

Aamna waved off the inconvenience. "Who knows when that'll arrive? Why stand around in the heat? Come on, I'll drop you home. And maybe get a glimpse of where you live—and finally meet your family."

Khadija responded carefully, "Thanks, but just drop me home. Skip the family introductions, please."

Aamna grinned, "Fine, fine—I won't crash your home. Just a ride. Hop in."

Scene 21

Beneath a Father's Shadow

When Professor Parker remained unreachable, Zafir decided it was time to speak with his father. He laid out everything—the research paper, the threats, the anonymous calls.

Stunned and deeply troubled, his father replied,

"I always thought your scientific pursuits were just a hobby. I never imagined they'd bring you this far… or that people would become a danger to your life."

Zafir responded quietly, "None of this would've happened if I hadn't published that research paper. That's where it all began. I still don't know who these people are, or what they ultimately want—but I can tell they're bold and ruthless. They fear neither law nor consequence."

His father took a breath, then said firmly,

"In that case, we must involve the police. I know Police Sheriff Peterson William personally. Let's explain the situation to him—I'm worried for your safety."

The sheriff listened carefully to their account and nodded.

"This is a small town. There are only a few ways in or out. I doubt they'll make any direct move here against Mr. Zafir. But for your peace of mind, I'll assign two officers to monitor him for the next thirty days. And if anything serious comes up, we can bring in the RCMP. No need to panic."

Scene 22

A Proposal Too Bright

Khadija was studying quietly in her room when one of her cousins—Liaqat's daughter—entered.

"You're being called to the drawing room."

Khadija looked up, puzzled. "Called... by whom?"

Already halfway out the door, the cousin replied,

"Taya Jan, Javed chacha, and Baba are all there. They're waiting for you."

Still unsure, Khadija walked into the drawing room. Her uncles were seated, their expressions warm and expectant.

"Come here, beti. Sit with us," her taya said gently.

As she settled down, Javed spoke,

"We've all agreed on something. Once you complete your intermediate exams, we want to send you abroad—for higher education in Turkey."

The words stunned Khadija. She looked from one face to another in disbelief.

"But... bade chacha, I haven't even finished my final exams yet. And how could I live all alone in a foreign country? I think I'll be fine studying here."

Liaqat jumped in, "Beti, we know we failed you before. Let us make up for it now. We'll take care of everything—your admission, your visa, housing, tuition—between the three of us. Your taya has several friends who run businesses in Turkey. The arrangements can all be managed."

Her taya added, "You don't need to worry at all. In fact, you may not know this—but it was your late father's deep wish to see you study abroad at a top institution."

It all felt strange, surreal. Khadija murmured,

"That's kind of you, but just the thought of leaving the country after my exams fills me with anxiety."

Javed smiled, "Leave the worry to us. I or Liaqat will travel with you, settle you in, make sure you're at ease—only then will we return. You'll never be left alone in this."

Her taya proposed, "Let's make things easier. I'll contact my friends in Turkey and get names and addresses of reputable universities. Liaqat, you handle the visas—for yourself and Khadija. Once she finishes her exams, we'll take her there to visit, and she can choose the university herself."

Khadija sat quietly, overwhelmed.

One half of her past had filled her ears with curses, and the other had drowned her dreams in silent neglect.

And now, suddenly—this: generosity, support, promises she never dared to imagine.

She couldn't tell if it was grace... or just another test in disguise.

Scene 23

The Line in the Sand

After speaking with the sheriff, Zafir had felt a flicker of peace. Two plainclothes officers were now assigned to monitor him discreetly. But one afternoon, his phone rang—and no number appeared.

He instantly knew it had come via the internet or a masked VPN route.

Zafir hesitated, thumb hovering over the screen. Then he answered.

It was him.

"You blocked my number and now you're trying to disappear. Did you really think ignoring me would make me go away?"

Zafir steadied his breath. "I don't want anything to do with you. Please don't call me again."

The man laughed—a slow, venomous sound.

"You've grown bold, haven't you? Denying me outright. Do you know what that decision will cost?"

But this time, Zafir didn't shrink.

"Do whatever you feel like. I've made my decision—I won't work for you. Don't call again."

There was a hiss like a serpent's breath before the threat came:

"I'll give you until tomorrow. If your answer remains no—then you alone will be responsible for what follows."

With that, the call ended.

Zafir's hands trembled as he immediately called the police. They assured him they'd trace the number.

"Don't worry," the officer said. "We're nearby and watching closely."

Scene 24

Between Gratitude and Guardedness

“Wow! That’s big news. But... why Turkey?” Aamna said, clearly intrigued as Khadija shared the news of possibly pursuing higher studies abroad.

“I mean, there’ll be a language barrier, won’t there? People don’t usually speak English there.”

Khadija nodded thoughtfully.

“It all feels a bit strange to me too. I don’t fully understand it. But my family is insistent I continue my education there after my intermediate exams.”

Aamna replied, “Honestly, it sounds really exciting to study abroad. But for a girl to live alone in a foreign country... well, my mom can’t even imagine it. Both of my sisters moved abroad, but only after they got married. Your family must be really open-minded about all this.”

Khadija answered in a quiet, uncertain tone,

“My younger uncle is taking me to Istanbul at the end of this month to show me some universities. As soon as my results are announced, they plan to enrol me and send me there.”

Aamna looked at her closely.

“That’s... unusual. But what’s bothering you so much? Surely your parents wouldn’t make a bad decision for you.”

Khadija gently corrected her.

“I live with my eldest uncle.”

“Oh... and your parents?” Aamna asked, caught off guard.

Khadija's voice was numb, detached.

"My father passed away. My mother lives in Sharjah with her second husband and their children."

Aamna's expression shifted.

"That explains why you always hesitated when we talked about family. I'm so sorry, Khadija. But honestly—you're lucky your uncles and their family take care of you. I know of a family in my own relatives who made life hell for their orphaned niece."

Khadija nodded softly.

"Yes... they've never made me feel unwanted."

Aamna smiled warmly.

"And if your uncle is doing so much for you—even considering sending you abroad—that says a lot. That's a blessing, yaar."

Scene 25

Shadows Need Stillness

Even after speaking to the police, Zafir's anxiety remained unshaken. But that afternoon, a message blinked on his phone—it was from Professor Parker.

"I was hospitalized due to illness and couldn't respond earlier. I'll be free to talk between six and six-thirty this evening. Let's speak then."

Relieved, Zafir resumed his work until evening, when he called and explained everything—the call, the threat, his mounting fear.

"Sir, what would you advise in this situation?" he asked.

Professor Parker's voice was calm but serious.

"I hadn't imagined things would escalate like this. Whoever this man is, it's clear he isn't genuinely interested in your innovation. If he were, he would've approached a major university or senior scientists, not threatened a young researcher. No—his goal isn't creation… it's control. He either wants you to fail or bind your work exclusively to him."

"I don't quite follow, sir," Zafir admitted.

"Don't fight fire with fire. Don't threaten him with police. Just do this one thing," Parker said.

"What's that, sir?"

"Tell him that living in Iqaluit and your personal constraints make it impossible to conduct further research. Say you lack the environment, the facilities, the capacity. Let him believe the idea has died on the vine." Professor Parker suggested.

Zafir thought for a moment. "I could say that... but will he believe me?"

Parker chuckled faintly. "Probably not. That's why he'll monitor you for a while. But if you stay still—stay quiet—he'll lose interest and move on."

"Alright, sir," Zafir said, absorbing the weight of it. "I'll try it—and keep you updated."

"Good," Parker replied. "And one more thing. When the time is right... do not give up on your idea. The world needs minds like yours."

Zafir closed his eyes for a moment. Then nodded slowly.

"Okay, sir. Thank you."

Scene 26

A Passport to Uncertainty

"Here you go, beti—your passport," Javed said, handing it over with a smile. "Your Turkish visa has been issued. You'll be leaving next week with Liaqat. With help from one of your taya's friends, we've shortlisted four universities—three in Istanbul, one in Trabzon. Go, see the campuses, tour the hostels, and choose the one that feels right. Once you're back and finish your intermediate exams, we'll begin preparations in earnest."

Khadija took the passport slowly.

"Thank you, bade chacha... but I'll say it again—I'd honestly prefer to continue my studies here."

Javed replied gently, "And I'll say it again—it was your late father's dream that his daughter receive the best education, from abroad."

Khadija nodded with restrained acceptance.

"Alright. When's the flight?"

"Liaqat will be here tonight. He'll explain the itinerary," Javed replied.

After they left the room, Khadija sat holding the passport—a small document that suddenly carried the weight of continents. For a fleeting moment, she thought about calling her mother in Sharjah. Sharing the news, maybe... maybe even asking for advice.

But that thought faded just as quickly.

Their bond wasn't strong enough. The silences were too wide. The warmth had long since cooled.

And so, Khadija placed the passport quietly on her bedside table—like a gift she wasn't sure she wanted.

Scene 27

The Silence of Steel

That evening, Zafir left the office on his bicycle, the cold Iqaluit air brushing past him. Cars were rare here, and paved roads even rarer. His mind, still heavy with unease, wandered as he pedalled toward home.

But then—two men blocked his path.

One of them, his face cold and expressionless, slipped a pistol halfway out of his coat pocket.

"Come with us. Silently. One wrong move—and it's over."

Zafir's heart pounded. He quickly glanced around, searching for the two plainclothes officers who had been assigned to shadow him.

But there was no one in sight.

He had no choice but to follow. The men led him to a nearby warehouse—empty, dimly lit, echoing with silence. Inside, one held him at gunpoint while the other spoke.

"You thought we were bluffing. That we bark but never bite."

Zafir's eyes darted again, hoping—praying—that the officers would appear, that someone had noticed. But the warehouse held only shadows.

The second man sneered.

"Looking for your police friends? We twisted the right arms. They're sitting quietly now—with their tails between their legs. Maybe now you understand how long our reach really is."

Zafir swallowed hard. "Wh-what do you want?"

The man's voice sharpened to a blade.

"Either you build the invention—for us. Or you build it for no one. And to guarantee that you don't build it for anyone else… we'll have to remove you from the equation."

Scene 28

Beneath Foreign Skies

Outside Istanbul's international airport, Khadija sat in a taxi beside her uncle Liaqat, absorbing the unfamiliar rhythm of a new land.

"Chhote Chacha," she asked hesitantly, "are we going straight to the university from here?"

Liaqat explained the plan, voice calm and reassuring.

"Not today, beta. We're heading to the hotel first. Tomorrow morning, we'll visit the three universities here in Istanbul, one by one—along with their hostels. The next day, we'll fly to Trabzon to visit the fourth university and return that same night. Then it's back to Pakistan the day after."

Anxiety bubbled in Khadija's chest. "But how will I manage here on my own, Chhote Chacha? People don't speak English here."

Liaqat gently reassured her. "These drivers and locals aren't well-educated, but in university you won't face much trouble. And if the language feels like a barrier, you can always enrol in a Turkish language course to help with daily communication."

But the weight in Khadija's chest didn't lift.

Sensing this, Liaqat added softly, "Don't worry, beti. Whichever university you like, we'll arrange for your admission there. No pressure."

Khadija nodded, eyes gazing out the taxi window at the blur of a city she didn't know whether to fear or embrace.

Scene 29

Captive Within the Spark

Trapped in the dim warehouse, the pistol still trained on him, Zafir heard the man speak coldly:

"And if you dare call that old professor again—or mention us—you won't survive. And neither will he. That old man's practically got one foot in the grave… all we need is a gentle push."

Terror swept over Zafir. Voice shaking, he said,

"F-Fine. I'll work for you. But inventions don't happen overnight. I'll need more research, resources… a proper lab."

The man laughed menacingly.

"You technical types always talk in circles. We're not here for theories—we're bounty hunters. Just tell us, in simple words, what you need."

Now Zafir's mind began to calculate. Slowly, he replied,

"I need scientific books and access to technical journals… materials for a prototype… and a fully equipped lab. But most of all—I need time and peace. If I'm staring down a gun barrel, I won't be able to work."

One of them made a phone call. Then he turned to Zafir.

"Write it all down. This warehouse is yours now. We'll build your lab here. Anything you need—will be brought here."

The other added,

"From now on, you'll live here until the invention is complete. No leaving, no communication with anyone—unless we approve it and control how it happens."

Shaken, Zafir protested,

"But this could take months… even years. How can I stay cut off from everything and everyone?"

"We make the rules," the man growled. "No outside contact. Period."

Zafir tried another plea,

"My parents… my family. They'll panic if I vanish. At least let me tell them I'll be unavailable."

"Too risky," the man snapped. "You'll stay hidden and work in silence."

"Then at least let me speak to my sister," Zafir said. "She doesn't live here. I won't tell her anything."

The men exchanged glances. Then, one relented.

"Fine. One short call. But if you slip—she goes down with you."

Using an encrypted VPN, the man placed the call and handed over the phone.

Saira's voice came through, full of warmth.

"Assalam-o-Alaikum, bhai jaan. How are you?"

"Wa Alaikum assalam, Gudiya. I have to leave for the U.S. on urgent work. Please tell everyone I'm safe… but I won't be in contact for a while."

Confused, Saira asked,

"Wait—what? Are you okay?"

"Yes, yes. I'm fine. Everything's perfect. Don't worry," Zafir replied, heart pounding.

She didn't buy it.

"Bhai jaan… I can hear it in your voice. What's really going on?"

"Nothing, Gudiya," he said softly. "I just… I miss sitting with you on that bench by the lake. That's all. Take care. Khuda Hafiz."

After the call, the man looked suspicious.

"That bit about the lake… what was that?"

"Just childhood memories," Zafir muttered. "Now, can you get me some stationery? And have this place cleaned—set it up properly. I'll draft the list of what I need."

The man nodded.

"It'll be done. And for your information, armed guards will be stationed here soon. So don't even think of escaping."

Zafir, now snapping back to composure, said crisply,

"Iqaluit's too small. It's not like I could disappear even if I wanted to. I'll work for you—but I need peace. And I don't want to see either of your faces while I do it."

The man grimaced.

"Fine. You'll get what you asked for. We'll be nearby… watching."

Scene 30

From Dust to Dawn

Khadija had chosen Avrasya University in Trabzon.

As she and Liaqat settled into their seats on the return flight to Pakistan, he turned to her with a contented smile.

"You made a good choice. Trabzon is a beautiful, peaceful little town. And the university is new and private—so the facilities and education will be excellent."

Khadija hesitated.

"But Chhote Chacha, its tuition fees are higher than the ones we saw in Istanbul."

Liaqat waved off the concern.

"Don't worry about the cost—we'll manage it. What matters is that you liked the university and the city. Once your intermediate is complete, we'll send you there."

Khadija sat back, quietly overwhelmed.

Just a few years ago, her maternal relatives had halted her education after school. Life then had been stitched with rejection and humiliation.

And now—here she was, flying home after choosing a university in Turkey, with her uncle by her side and her dream neatly folded into a passport.

It felt surreal.

She didn't know if this new chapter would deliver peace or another twist in the tale—but for the first time in years, the door didn't look like a trap.

It looked like possibility.

Scene 31

Between Lines Unspoken

After speaking with Zafir, Saira couldn't shake her unease. His words had been stiff, hollow, and his tone—far too calm to be genuine. That kind of silence always meant trouble.

Later that night, she called home, expecting to hear that everything was fine. But instead, her mother answered, her voice heavy with worry.

"Your brother hasn't come home since evening," she said. "We've tried reaching him, but nothing. His phone's off."

Trying to calm the panic she now felt herself, Saira replied quickly,

"Mummy, he called me earlier. He said he's had to leave urgently for the U.S.—some important matter—and asked me to let you know he might not be in touch for a while."

Her mother's voice sharpened.

"He could've called us himself. We've been out of our minds with worry. Doesn't he understand that?"

Saira, gently covering for him, said,

"It's my fault, really. He told me to inform you—I just got caught up with work and forgot. Don't blame him."

But her mother wasn't convinced.

"You always defend him, just like when you were kids. No matter what he does. He should've called us directly. And what city did he go to? When will he return?"

Saira hesitated. "He didn't say. I tried calling back, but his phone's switched off. He could be in transit—or somewhere with no signal. I'll try him again tomorrow and let you know everything. Please don't worry. And tell Daddy not to stress either."

After hanging up, Saira's worry only deepened. She had assumed Zafir would have also informed their parents. That's why she'd waited to make the call herself. But now it was clear: something was truly wrong.

And the silence wasn't protecting anyone anymore.

Scene 32

The Silence Between Celebrations

After returning from Turkey, Khadija resumed college. Time marched on. She completed her second-year exams and now waited for her results.

One afternoon, her friend Aamna visited. After meeting Khadija's aunt and cousins, the two friends settled into Khadija's room.

Aamna beamed. "I have big news—I'm engaged! And the wedding's this year."

Khadija smiled warmly. "Congratulations. But isn't it a little soon?"

Aamna laughed. "Not really. I lost a year repeating matric, and another when we moved from Karachi to Islamabad. Things had gotten so bad in Karachi—my dad couldn't continue business there. So dear friend, I'm already nineteen. This isn't exactly rushed."

Khadija murmured, "My eighteenth birthday is next month. Never celebrated it before... and I don't think I will this time either."

Aamna grinned. "Then I'll bring cake. We'll celebrate together."

But Khadija replied quietly, "No, leave it. I've grown tired of borrowed joy... moments that don't truly belong to me."

Frustrated, Aamna said, "Why do you always close yourself off like this? I've never seen you laugh properly. Not once. I've told every joke I know, and all I get is a faint smile. Why are you so stingy with your emotions?"

Khadija's eyes fell to the floor.

"Happiness and I... we don't get along."

Scene 33

Signals in the Silence

By the next day, the warehouse had been partially transformed. A small office space was ready, and more supplies continued to arrive. Zafir took stock of the setup—and of reality. The surveillance was tight. Escape was out of the question. Reluctantly, he surrendered to the current—for now.

Meanwhile, Saira's fears had crystallized into certainty: something was terribly wrong.

After repeated failed calls, she finally rang her father and told him everything.

His voice was tight with frustration and worry.

"I had a feeling—he's always been tangled in these strange scientific obsessions. I never thought it would land him in real danger. When he didn't return home last night, I called the police sheriff. What he said made me uneasy—but when you told me Zafir had gone to the U.S., I was reassured. I thought maybe he'd just left in a hurry."

Saira pressed gently, "What exactly did the sheriff say?"

Her father exhaled sharply.

"They had placed him under police protection. But without any warning, they pulled those officers off. When I asked why, Sheriff Peterson gave a vague answer—something about manpower shortage. Now neither of us can reach him. If he was still in Nunavut or Iqaluit, maybe we could blame bad mobile signals. But in the U.S.? That doesn't add up."

"Daddy," Saira said firmly, "please speak with the sheriff again. Ask him to help us find Bhai jaan."

After a pause, her father replied,

"Yes… that's what I'll do. I'm heading to his office right now."

Scene 34

Where Faith Meets Fire

"So, what's new?" Aamna asked brightly over the phone.

"Nothing really," Khadija replied. "Just going over some books I brought from Turkey. What about you? Any plans to continue studying—or are you diving into wedding preparations now?"

Aamna chuckled. "Looks like studying ends here. The wedding's the main topic at home now—preparations have started. My sisters are planning to fly in, but they'll probably arrive just before the big day."

Khadija asked, "Will you be staying in Islamabad after marriage?"

"No, I'll be moving to Lahore," Aamna replied. "What about you—any proposals on the horizon?"

With quiet conviction, Khadija answered,

"I don't plan on getting married. Not now. Not ever."

Aamna paused, shocked. "What? Why not?"

Khadija replied, unfazed,

"Because I hate the very idea of what a husband becomes—a father. That entire species disgusts me."

Aamna was stunned. "Oh my God! Khadija—what are you saying?"

"It's how I feel. It's my private truth," Khadija said softly.

Aamna tried to reason with her. "Whatever may have happened… one bad experience doesn't mean every man in the world is untrustworthy. My father loves me dearly. I believe my husband will too. You need to learn to trust people, Khadija."

Khadija cut the conversation short. "This isn't about you. It's personal. Let's not get into it."

After a moment, Aamna said gently, "Okay. But as your friend—your only friend, really—can I ask you something?"

"Yes?" Khadija uttered.

"You seem angry at people... at fate. But are you angry at Allah too?"

Khadija looked confused. "What do you mean?"

Aamna looked straight into the question.

"I've never seen you pray or fast. These are basics of our faith. You are Muslim, aren't you?"

"I am," Khadija whispered.

"Then why no prayer, no fasting, no observance of *purdah* as prescribed?" Aamna questioned.

Khadija answered with painful honesty:

"I believe in Allah... but I don't obey Him. My grievance is this: Why me? Why was I denied love and respect? Other girls had fathers who cherished them. I only ever received anger. Their mothers nurtured them. Mine left me behind. I grew up among taunts and cruelty. Later I learned... my own father denied I was his daughter. Called me someone else's child. That lie buried me in shame and filth—until I found out he was mentally ill. Only in the last couple of years have I even begun to understand what self-worth feels like."

Aamna was quiet with compassion. "You never told me any of this. I'm sorry. I truly am."

Khadija remained silent, so Aamna spoke gently again,

"But Khadija—rebelling against Allah, holding on to anger… it'll never bring you peace. He is the Creator—we are merely His creation. No one finds shelter—here or in the Hereafter—by turning away from Him."

"What are you trying to say?" Khadija asked softly.

"You can't fight fate. What's written cannot be undone. But you can pray for ease and healing. Start honouring your spiritual duties—your prayers, your fasts. It's not for anyone else. It's for you."

Khadija's voice was flat. "I don't want to talk about it."

Scene 35

The Architects of Smoke

In a dimly lit room, a man sat silently, a cigarette glowing between his fingers. Smoke curled upward into the stale air. The phone on the desk buzzed.

"The task is done," said the voice on the other end. "What now?"

The man exhaled smoke slowly, his voice steady.

"Let Zafir work quietly. But keep the surveillance tight. No one can know he's working for us. All his communication will go through our secure channel. Nothing else."

The caller added,

"Our IT expert is on-site, managing the entire operation. But the boy's father has filed a report with the police. They're actively searching for him."

Snuffing out the cigarette in the ashtray, the man asked,

"I instructed you to prepare false travel documents. Is that done?"

"Yes," came the reply.

The man leaned back in his chair, the room thick with silence and smoke.

Scene 36

Echoes at the Gate

"Congratulations, Khadija! You got an A-One grade in your intermediate exams. That calls for a celebration!" Javed exclaimed with joy.

Her taya, who happened to be visiting, added enthusiastically,

"Absolutely! And I say we invite your maternal relatives too—let them see how bright our daughter is!"

Khadija quickly interjected,

"Thank you, Taya, but there's no need to invite anyone from my mother's side. I don't want to see them."

Liaqat, still beaming, said,

"Alright, we won't call them—but we should at least inform Arifah. We'll invite her. She should see how well you're doing with your paternal family."

Khadija opened her mouth to object again… but paused. The glow on their faces—their rare and radiant happiness—made it difficult to refuse.

So she stayed silent.

Scene 37

A Search Without a Map

After hearing the full account, Sheriff Peterson formally filed a missing person report.

"Since you believe he's gone to the U.S.," he said, "first we need to verify whether he actually left Iqaluit or disappeared locally."

He immediately contacted border security and requested the exit records—flights, ferry logs, and any departures in the past 48 hours.

Then he turned to Zafir's father.

"Go home for now. I'll update you as soon as I have something solid."

By evening, a call came from the sheriff's office. His voice was composed but cautious.

"According to records, Zafir departed yesterday afternoon—first to Vancouver, then on to Seattle."

"Oh..." was all his father could utter, the weight of confusion tightening in his chest.

Sheriff Peterson added,

"That suggests he left Iqaluit safely and went missing after reaching Seattle. I've already contacted Seattle PD. I'll update you as soon as they respond."

When Zafir's father returned home, his face told the story. Everyone there mirrored his concern—each of them haunted by the same question: Where could Zafir have gone... and why in such silence?

His mother, voice choked with fear, said,

"Please… go to Seattle yourself. Bring my son back."

Gravely, he nodded. "I'm thinking the same. But Seattle's a massive city. I'll wait to hear from the sheriff once more… then I'll go. Maybe I'll take Zakir or Shakir with me."

Scene 38

The Echo of an Open Wound

"My child, congratulations," Arifah said warmly on the phone. "I'm so happy your uncles are giving you the love and respect you've always deserved."

It was the day of the celebration, and Arifah had called Khadija after receiving the news.

Khadija replied softly,

"I'm going to Turkey for higher studies. Taya and Chhote Chacha arranged my admission."

Arifah sounded taken aback. "But why? You could continue your education right there in Pakistan. What's the need to go so far?"

Khadija's voice sharpened with a quiet rebellion.

"Because I want to. And if you have a problem with that, then I especially want to."

Arifah tried to soften the storm rising in her daughter's tone.

"My child... when will you forgive your mother? I love you so much. It breaks my heart to think of you in pain. Just don't go so far away. Stay there. Study there."

But Khadija's voice had already closed its doors.

"I've been admitted. And if there's one reason I won't cancel my plans—it's you. Please hang up before your dear husband Mr. Nasir gets upset."

Scene 39

Where the Trail Grows Cold

With contacts provided by the sheriff, Zafir's father—accompanied by his younger son Shakir—travelled to Seattle. At the local police station, officers cross-verified with border and airport security records.

"According to flight data, Zafir did arrive in Seattle. But where he went from the airport—or how he disappeared—we can't say yet," one officer explained.

"We'll file an official report. Please give us a clear photo of him. That'll help us pull CCTV footage from the airport and surrounding areas."

For a week, father and son stayed in Seattle, chasing thin leads and thinner hopes. Back home, they shared updates through scattered calls. Saira phoned often too, each time hoping, each time disappointed.

But no clue surfaced. No trace.

Eventually, burdened by silence, they returned to Iqaluit—empty-handed and heavy-hearted.

At home, the atmosphere was thick with dread. Zafir's mysterious disappearance in a foreign land had brought darkness to every corner. Their minds spiralled with haunting possibilities.

In Winnipeg, Saira sat restlessly, eyes tired from weeping. Her husband Kashif gently asked,

"Think carefully… during your last conversation, did Zafir say anything—even something small—that hinted at why or where he was going?"

Saira shook her head slowly.

"No… he said nothing."

Kashif pressed gently,

"If something shady was happening, surely he may have given some kind of clue—even unintentionally."

Tears streamed down her face.

"I don't know… I just don't know. Ya Allah, keep Bhai jaan safe—wherever he is."

Scene 40

The Unexpected Inheritance

Javed knocked gently at the door.

"Beta, may I come in?"

"Yes, bade chacha. Please." Khadija set her book aside.

He stepped in, holding some papers.

"These need your signature. They're forms for the university and the embassy."

Khadija signed them without question. Then Javed pulled out another set.

"These are legal documents—some court papers. These also need your signature."

Khadija frowned slightly.

"What are these for, bade chacha?"

Javed explained,

"They relate to a small property your late father, Ramzan, left in your name. We want to ensure the transfer is official before you leave for Turkey."

Khadija blinked in surprise.

"Property?"

He nodded.

"Just a small shop, and a few hundred thousands locked in a bank account. Once you sign these, everything becomes yours. Don't worry—we don't want a single rupee from it. You're our responsibility, and this is rightfully yours."

Khadija took the documents, her voice low.

"That's not what I meant, chacha. I'll sign."

She signed each page, carefully. Javed collected the papers into a file, visibly pleased.

"Start preparing now. This time, your taya himself will take you to Turkey and help settle you into the hostel."

"Alright," Khadija replied quietly.

He added warmly,

"And don't worry. Your taya has many contacts there. If anything goes wrong, you call them—or us. We're always here."

Khadija gave a small nod. She didn't say it aloud, but something inside her stirred—perhaps not joy, not yet. But something close.

Scene 41

Shadows with Supply Chains

Three weeks into captivity, Zafir finally approached one of the handlers.

"To begin prototyping, I need to run preliminary experiments. For that, I need materials."

The man nodded dismissively. "Fine. Make a list. I'll get it shipped from the neighbouring country."

Zafir narrowed his eyes.

"It's not stuff you grab from a super store. The kind of equipment I need—well, let me put it this way: one item alone is military-grade titanium. Highly regulated. Requires disclosure of who's using it and how. It's not just rare—it's scrutinized."

The man clearly didn't follow. He placed a call, muttered something, then handed the phone to Zafir.

"We're connecting you with one of our Chinese suppliers. Tell him what you need—he'll deliver."

A voice answered in heavily accented English:

"What you need?"

Zafir replied evenly,

"Military-grade titanium. Industrial 3D printer. Drones. A high-speed frequency generator. That's the beginning."

The voice remained monotone. "All can be arranged. Which kind of drone?"

"Can you get military-grade models?" Zafir asked cautiously.

"If the money's good—anything is possible."

"Then I'll need three military-grade drones."

"Everything will be delivered within two weeks."

Startled, Zafir asked, "Two weeks? Seriously? Where?"

The voice replied coldly,

"The people you're working for know where it's going. And how to get it in… without customs or security sniffing it. If you need anything else—tell me by tomorrow morning."

With that, the line went dead.

And Zafir stood frozen, realizing he'd just stepped into a machine far bigger—and darker—than he'd imagined.

Scene 42

Where the Horizon Opens

Trabzon was a small yet breath-taking town nestled beside the Black Sea, some 1,100 kilometres from Istanbul. Its four large lakes shimmered at the foot of the surrounding mountains—a postcard of serenity.

After a two-hour flight from Istanbul, Khadija and her taya landed in Trabzon at around 7:00 p.m.

"We'll visit your hostel tomorrow," her taya said as they stepped outside the terminal. "For tonight, let's check into a hotel. Tomorrow morning I'll get you settled, and then I'll head back."

They booked adjoining rooms at a luxurious five-star hotel—The Royal Comfort Hotel—perched by the edge of the Black Sea. The view was as poetic as its name promised.

When Khadija entered her room, she walked out onto the terrace and paused. The vast sweep of the sea glistened under the twilight sky, its waves whispering against the stone shore.

She stood still, as if daring herself to believe this moment was real.

Life, she mused, is a strange thing. One moment, you're drowning in despair... and the next, you're soaring through altitudes you never imagined.

Scene 43

A Message Hidden in Memory

Saira was at home, lost in thought, her mind circling around her brother Zafir. And then—suddenly—something flashed in her memory like a bolt of lightning.

It was a phrase he had said during their last call:

"I'm fine, Gudiya. I just can't talk much right now. But today, I'm really missing sitting with you on that bench by the lake. Take care. Allah Hafiz."

She whispered to herself, "Why did he mention the lake like that—completely out of context?"

She fell into thought, then muttered aloud,

"Oh... that was a sign. A clue that he's in trouble."

Since childhood, whenever Zafir was deeply troubled or overwhelmed, he would go sit by the lake. It was his retreat.

"Does this mean... he's actually still near that lake? Still in Iqaluit—not in Seattle?"

She quickly called her father and shared everything. He replied cautiously,

"But dear, he took a flight to Seattle and never returned. How could he still be here?"

Saira, with growing certainty, insisted,

"No, Daddy. Mentioning the lake wasn't random. I didn't see it then, but now I'm sure—he was trying to tell me something. He's here. He's somewhere near the lake in Iqaluit."

Her father paused, thinking deeply.

"If that's true… we never even searched here. We've spent all this time looking in Seattle. I need to speak with the sheriff again—immediately."

Scene 44

Between Dawn and Distance

Khadija woke early. After freshening up, she stepped out onto the terrace, where the Black Sea gleamed softly below. From one edge of the sky, the sun was rising—its golden fingers unfurling across the water.

The quiet was perfect, yet her mind stirred.

Aamna's words from days ago echoed in her thoughts:

"Allah is the Creator... and we are His creation. We have no right to question Him."

Khadija folded her arms, her gaze distant. The beauty before her offered peace—yet her soul tugged in silent debate with faith.

Just then, a knock at the door startled her.

She assumed it must be her taya. When she opened it, it was a hotel bellboy.

"Yes?" Khadija asked in English.

The bellboy spoke in Turkish:

"Odanda kahvaltı sever misin? yoksa restorana mı gideceksin?"

("Madam, would you like breakfast in your room or down in the restaurant?")

Khadija blinked. She couldn't understand.

"What are you saying?" she asked again in English, a bit puzzled.

Smiling politely, the bellboy replied:

"İngilizce bilen birini arıyorum."

("I'll call someone who speaks English.")

Then he left.

Khadija closed the door and sat back on her bed. Maybe she should knock on taya's door next door, wake him up… but then she paused.

What if he's still asleep? Let him rest.

She'd wait.

And quietly… begin to adjust.

Scene 45

Strings from the Shadows

In a dimly lit room, a man sat smoking, his face lost in haze. His phone rang. A voice on the other end reported:

"He's been provided with everything he asked for."

The man took a slow drag, then exhaled.

"Now engineer a reason for him to call Professor Parker. I want to know exactly how far he's progressed—and what he's truly working on."

The caller hesitated. "Professor Parker?"

The man smiled—coldly.

"Yes. The professor is on our payroll. It was through his guidance—and manipulation—that the boy was brought into our fold. Zafir trusts him completely. That's the leverage we'll keep exploiting."

Scene 46

The Disappearing Horizon

Back in her room, Khadija returned to the terrace. The sea stretched endlessly before her, calm and glistening. But the scenes playing in her mind were anything but serene.

Memories drifted to the men in her life—her biological father, her stepfather, her uncles from her mother's side… and how vastly different they were from her paternal uncles.

If it hadn't been for her uncles—Taya and Chhote Chacha—she might still be stuck at her maternal relatives' home, enduring their scolding and slights. They had lifted her up when no one else would.

As she lingered in those thoughts, the doorbell rang again.

Probably the same hotel staff again, she muttered, annoyed. If it's the same guy, I'm calling Taya. I can't understand a single word he says.

But when she opened the door, she was met by two men. One was the same bellboy. The other—a man in a sharp suit—spoke in fluent English.

"Good morning, ma'am. I'm the hotel manager. We just wanted to ask: before checkout, would you prefer breakfast in your room or in the restaurant downstairs?"

Khadija's eyes widened. "Checkout? My Taya would know that. He's in the room next door. I'll just ask him—"

But as she turned to knock on the adjoining door, the manager interrupted gently.

"Ma'am… if you're referring to the gentleman who booked both rooms—he's no longer there. He checked out very early this morning. He had a morning flight. He left instructions that the guest in the neighbouring room would check out after breakfast."

Khadija's heart lurched.

"W-What do you mean he left? He couldn't have… not without me. There's some mistake."

She moved toward the next room's doorbell, but the manager held up a hand calmly.

"Please, ma'am. Why would I mislead you? Step aside—I have the master key. I'll show you."

Scene 47

Whispers Beneath Steel Doors

"My warehouse had been shut for over a year," the man explained to the sheriff during questioning at the station. "That party paid an entire year's rent in advance. I have no idea what they're doing in there."

The sheriff leaned forward, tone more cautious than accusatory.

"I've received some information suggesting clandestine activity inside that warehouse. Armed guards are stationed outside. We've even received instructions from higher up not to interfere. But this concerns a missing person—and we have reason to believe that location may be involved. That's why we summoned you."

The man shrugged, unimpressed.

"All I know is that a company—registered in New York—rented my warehouse. What they do is none of my business. I'm just relieved the place finally brought in some income."

The sheriff nodded curtly.

"Alright. You can go. Thank you."

Once the man left, the sheriff immediately placed a call.

"Do we have the forensic analysis on Zafir's mobile data?"

He listened for a moment, then said:

"Hmm... looks like there are only a few numbers he frequently contacted. One is his sister. The rest are family landlines. This one belongs to a Professor

Parker Smith. And then there are a few incoming calls from unidentified numbers."

He hung up and muttered under his breath:

"That means we'll need to check into Professor Parker. But it's outside our jurisdiction... I'll need to contact the Texas Police Chief."

Scene 48

The Vanishing Point

The manager unlocked the room, and Khadija rushed inside, scanning every corner—but her taya was gone.

Fear rising in her chest, she stammered,

"W-Where did my taya go?"

The manager replied gently,

"Ma'am, as I said—he checked out during the early hours. Could you please let us know whether you'll have your breakfast here in the room or—"

Before he could finish, Khadija interrupted,

"I need to make a phone call."

"Of course," the manager said. "You may use the room phone. Just note that any calls will be billed at checkout, since both rooms were prepaid."

Then turning to the bellboy, he added,

"Bring breakfast to the room, please."

Once they left, Khadija stood frozen. Time seemed suspended, as if reality itself were pausing to make sense of what had just happened.

Taya? Gone? How could he leave without saying a word? What was she supposed to do now?

She stumbled back into her room, sat on the edge of the bed, and buried her head in her hands—confused, shaken, alone.

Scene 49

Ashes Before the Fall

Zafir was working intently in the lab, scribbling notes, his eyes darting between readouts and circuit boards. But then—something shifted.

Muffled voices. Rapid footsteps. A ripple of panic.

Suddenly, one of the men burst in, eyes wide with urgency.

"We have to go—now! Grab what you can!"

Before Zafir could react, others had stormed in, snatching hard drives, toolkits, and blueprints. The man grabbed Zafir by the arm.

"You're coming too. The police are outside. We're torching this place before they breach it—nothing must remain."

They rushed him out the rear exit where delivery trucks usually came and went. A black, unmarked van stood waiting. Zafir was shoved inside, the back doors slammed shut behind him. The air inside pulsed with dread.

Then came the noise—panic rising from within the building. Yells, footsteps, the distant roar of flames. A phone buzzed.

One man answered, listened, and relayed in a clipped voice:

"Fire's set. The lab and office are burning. By the time the police enter, every trace will be ash. You're clear to move now—their entire focus is at the front gate."

Zafir's chest tightened. Whatever he'd been part of—whatever control he thought he had—was gone. Now, there was only escape… and smoke.

Scene 50

Without Anchor

A little while later, the same hotel staffer returned, set the breakfast trolley inside, and quietly left.

But Khadija couldn't taste a thing.

Her appetite had deserted her, as had her ability to make sense of anything. Her mind spun in circles, looking for even one fixed point.

"My Pakistani phone probably won't work here..." she thought desperately. "But if I can just retrieve Chacha's number from it, I can call him—he'll explain everything."

She looked around for her handbag. It wasn't on the nightstand. It wasn't on the chair. Her heart tightened.

"Where's my bag?" She stood up, scanning the room again—and then it hit her.

"Last night... Taya had said, 'Leave your bag with me. I'll organize your documents and forms for tomorrow so you don't face any trouble at the university.'"

The memory struck like cold water.

That bag had her passport. Her money. Her phone. Everything.

She sat down, clutching her head, eyes wide with alarm.

The view outside was still breath-taking. But inside—her world had begun to collapse.

Scene 51

Smoke Without a Trace

That evening, the police sheriff sat down with Zafir's father for a private conversation.

"We strongly suspect Zafir was being held captive right there by those people," the sheriff said gravely. "But we found no evidence of what they were actually doing. By the time we conducted the raid, the place was already on fire. More than half the warehouse was in flames. No one was inside—and the private guards at the gate claimed they knew nothing about what went on within."

Zafir's father shook his head in alarm.

"So that means… they set the fire themselves? Covered their tracks and escaped with Zafir?"

"Seems that way," the sheriff replied. "But what's now certain is—they're still here, in Nunavut. Possibly even still in Iqaluit. Slipping out unnoticed won't be easy. We've already alerted the coast guards and airport security. They won't get far."

Zafir's father let out a weary sigh.

"Thank you. I just want my son back safely. I appreciate you standing by our old friendship."

The sheriff looked at him firmly.

"I had my suspicions the moment pressure started coming down from higher up. But we're here to serve and protect the public—not to bow to unjust orders. Don't worry. My entire team is fully committed to solving this case."

Scene 52

Borrowed Hours

Khadija didn't have a single phone number memorized. All she had now was a suitcase full of clothes and a small trolley bag. Panic swelled again—what was she supposed to do?

Just then, a knock at the door.

She opened it cautiously. The hotel manager stood there again. Glancing at the untouched breakfast trolley, he said politely,

"Madam, this was a continental breakfast. Perhaps you didn't like it? If you'd prefer something else—Oriental or Asian, maybe—I can send that instead."

Khadija didn't know what to say. Her silence lingered too long.

Sensing her confusion, the manager added,

"Actually, I came to ask when you'll be checking out. The gentleman you arrived with technically completed checkout already—both rooms were under his name. We just need to prepare this room for the next guest."

Khadija's voice faltered,

"Can I stay a little longer?"

The manager smiled politely.

"Of course. Regular checkout is at 1 p.m. He just checked out unusually early. You're welcome to stay for another hour or two. It's 8:30 now—so checking out by 10 would be perfectly fine."

Scene 53

The Light of Conviction

It was night-time. The air in Winnipeg was cool, heavy with unease. Saira sat at the edge of her bed, prayer beads slipping through her fingers, glancing at the clock every few minutes. Finally, unable to wait any longer, she picked up her phone and called her father.

He answered in a tired but steadied voice.

"My dear, your hunch was absolutely right. You understood Zafir's signal perfectly."

Saira's breath caught.

"R-Really? Do you mean…?"

"We're now quite certain he was being held in that warehouse. By the time we raided it, it was already burning. They destroyed everything and vanished—but your insight has shifted everything." He responded.

Saira's eyes welled up.

" I knew it meant something. Daddy, just pray now—pray that Bhai jaan comes back to us safe and sound."

Her father's voice grew soft, edged with emotion.

"I'm praying every moment, beta. And I'm proud of you—you saw what no one else did. You heard the truth hidden between his words."

Saira's tears now came freely, but her voice was calm.

" May Allah protect him, wherever he is, and bring him back to us soon."

The night remained still—but within it, bloomed a fragile sense of hope.

Scene 54

Whispers Through Wooden Walls

Zafir and the equipment had been transported to a small farm ranch—an old wooden summer house once owned by a family, now deserted in the harsh winter. The property had only two rooms, a small kitchen, and a narrow lounge.

The captors locked Zafir in one of the rooms. They assumed he was out of earshot, unaware that the thin wooden walls whispered their conversation back to him.

Outside, two men stood speaking in hushed urgency.

One muttered, “Still don’t get how the police found out about the warehouse.”

The other waved it off. “Forget that. Focus on the priority—we need to hide this equipment in a secure place and vanish. We’ll come back for it later when things cool down.”

The first asked grimly, “What about the boy?”

The second one’s voice turned cold. “He should’ve been eliminated already. But the boss wants him alive—for now. Until we know exactly how far he got with his research.”

The first man frowned. “But how are we supposed to know that? We don’t get this scientific stuff.”

The second man smirked cruelly.

“That’s what the boss’s pawn is for—Professor Parker. We’ll get the boy to talk to him. The professor will extract everything we need to know. After that… we dispatch the boy up.”

Zafir froze. He couldn't believe what he had just heard.

Professor Parker… the same man who had been his mentor, his guide… the one he had trusted.

And now—he's the one holding the blade behind his back.

Fear clawed at his gut—not just of betrayal, but of death. He needed a plan. He needed a way out. Fast.

Scene 55

The Cost of Betrayal

As soon as he stepped out of the airport, Khadija's taya's phone rang.

"Yes, I've landed in Islamabad," he said calmly.

It was Javed on the line.

"Liaqat is with me too. So? Have you left her there?"

Taya replied,

"Yes. I've got all the documents, her phone, and the money with me. I'll be home in half an hour—we'll talk then."

Once home, the three brothers gathered in a closed drawing room. Javed began:

"Alright, time to settle the accounts."

But Liaqat raised a concern.

"Before that, something's bothering me. Javed bhai, the first set of papers Khadija signed had three shop deeds. But the ones signed after she turned eighteen only mention two. What happened to the third?"

Javed laughed it off.

"You're so impatient. The third deed was with her—we now have it too. The first papers weren't even valid because she was a minor. The latest ones include her CNIC number. I've already spoken to the lawyer—legally we're all clear now."

Taya handed over a file.

"Here's the third shop deed. A property dealer has already agreed to sell everything quickly. Leaving her stranded over there was part of the plan. She doesn't know the language, and locals won't understand her either. That's why we sent her to a remote town instead of Istanbul or Ankara—she'll just drift helplessly for a while. That gives us a couple of weeks' buffer."

Javed added,

"By then, we'll have sold everything and split the money. Even if she returns, there'll be nothing left."

Liaqat asked uneasily,

"But what if she does come back?"

Taya said coldly,

"Then we'll hand her over to a shelter. She has no idea what her father owned anyway."

Liaqat pressed again,

"So let's do the math."

Javed recited like reading an inventory:

"One house, one flat, three shops—total estimated value: 260 million rupees. Plus another 42 million stuck in the bank, now legally transferred to Khadija's personal account, which she shares jointly—with me."

Taya concluded:

"So roughly 302 million. We'll divide it three ways—33% each. Now focus on selling everything quickly. The power of attorney is in my name. Tell the dealer to start immediately."

Liaqat nodded.

"My property agent is sharp. We'll wrap this up in a week. But one thing still confuses me—why all this drama? Couldn't we have done it more easily?"

Javed smirked.

"If a deal had stalled and someone asked to meet the real owner—how could we present Khadija? This way, we're airtight legally. And we can prove she's abroad for studies. Won't be back for years."

Taya, justifying their deceit, added smoothly:

"And besides… Arifa walked away from Ramzan herself. He never acknowledged Khadija in his life. How could we let her own everything after his death?"

Javed agreed with a twisted smirk.

"And Khadija never thought highly of Bhai Ramzan anyway—so what right does she have to inherit his legacy?"

Scene 56

A Bluff Between Life and Death

Zafir was torn. Should he try to escape… or wait? He didn't have long to dwell—the door suddenly unlocked and one of the guards stepped in.

"There's a phone call for you. Talk. But if you say a word about us—you're finished."

They handed him the phone.

"Hello?" Zafir said cautiously.

Professor Parker's voice came from the other end, warm and concerned:

"Oh, hello dear! Thank God you're alright. It took a lot of effort and strings to get through to the higher-ups—but I finally tracked you down. Are you safe?"

Zafir, inwardly bitter, thought, "Sir, you've mastered acting just as well as science."

Aloud, he spoke slowly,

"I'm physically fine, sir… but I'm being held captive."

Parker responded quickly,

"Don't worry—I've involved some very influential people. I'm doing everything I can to get them to release you."

"Thank you," Zafir said, masking his distrust.

Then Parker, in a seemingly casual tone, asked:

"One thing I've been wondering—had you made any practical progress on the invention yet? Or were you still in the early research phase?"

Zafir immediately recognized the trap. The answer could decide his fate.

He lowered his voice and replied,

"Sir... the initial computer simulations had reached ninety percent accuracy, and I'd completed about ten percent of the lab modelling. But during the raid, these idiots burned everything—including my entire body of work."

"Oh... I see," Parker muttered. "Well, when you're safe and things calm down, let's pick it back up together."

Zafir added nervously,

"But sir, these people... they seem dangerous. Ruthless."

Parker reassured him,

"Don't worry. I'm in contact with the people who matter. Everything will be fine."

The call ended. A guard took the phone from Zafir, relocked the door, and left.

Alone again, Zafir sat with a racing heart.

It was a bluff.

But if it worked—if they believed he had something too valuable to lose—they wouldn't kill him. At least, not yet.

And it worked.

After Parker's report, the captors dropped their plan to eliminate Zafir. A new order came down: intimidate him, extract him from Iqaluit, and move him to Texas—where under Parker's direct supervision, he would complete the research.

Scene 57

Toward Shelter, Not Safety

Khadija sat anxiously, unable to eat despite her hunger. Her thoughts swirled. Where will I go with just my luggage?

Then it struck her—the hostel. Maybe it would at least offer a roof over her head.

But she didn't know the address. She had no money. All she knew was the name: Avrasya University. And her mind kept circling back to the same question—Why did Taya leave so suddenly? Without a word?

At 10 a.m., the hotel manager returned. Before he could speak, Khadija blurted out:

"My passport, my money, all my documents—they're missing. The uncle I came with... just disappeared. I was admitted to Avrasya University. I came here from Pakistan to study... and now I'm stuck in this mess."

The manager didn't grasp everything she said—but it was clear the girl in front of him was frightened, stranded, and alone.

He thought for a moment and replied gently:

"Ma'am, I'm afraid you'll still need to vacate the room by our usual checkout time. I can let you stay until then, but not longer. I do understand you're in some trouble... but I have limitations too."

Khadija took a breath.

"My family arranged accommodation at the university hostel. Could you—please—help get me there? I have no money at all. Once I reach the hostel, I'll try to contact my family and figure out what's going on."

The manager paused, then nodded.

"Alright. I'll call the hotel shuttle. It can drop you off at the university hostel."

Scene 58

Through Ice and Intrigue

In Iqaluit, police continued to search for Zafir in every possible direction, but so far, they had no leads. His family remained engulfed in anxiety and fear.

The next morning, his captors came into the room and dragged him out. One of them, his voice gruff, said:

"God knows what that old professor sees in you. But we've got orders from above—you're being moved to the U.S., to him. Problem is, we can't use normal routes. The police have everything locked down."

Zafir blinked, alarmed.

"W-What do you mean by that?"

The man snapped,

"We can't fly out. Airport security's crawling with police. Boat's our only option. Ice has melted enough this time of year. But we've been informed the coast guards are watching all passenger jetties."

Having grown up in Iqaluit, Zafir knew: the only safe way out of the city was by air. There were no roads in or out. The sea remained frozen most of the year, and only during July and August did the coastal routes briefly thaw enough for small passenger boats. Even then, crossing the bay was risky. Only powerful icebreaker ships could cut through the glacial water year-round—and those were reserved for cargo.

To attempt an escape now, by sea, was to gamble with death.

Tense, Zafir replied,

"You're not from here—I've lived here my whole life. What you're planning is dangerous. The sea's freezing cold, littered with icebergs, and there are no defined paths. You're risking your lives—and mine."

The man, unfazed, explained flatly,

"We've made arrangements. There's a large icebreaker stationed in Hudson Bay. We'll take a small boat from a deserted coast, reach the bay, and board it. In two days, we'll be near Manitoba's coastline. From there, we take a small boat to the town of Churchill, then catch a flight to Winnipeg. After that—next flight to Austin, Texas. That's where you'll meet Professor Parker."

Zafir listened, dread tightening around his chest.

The plan was reckless.

But they were deadly serious.

Scene 59

Doors Closed Too Soon

Khadija stepped out of the hotel shuttle, her suitcase and trolley bag trailing behind her, and walked up to the main gate of the hostel. She had been here before with her younger uncle—at least now she knew the way. Without hesitation, she made her way to the reception office.

"Good morning," she said softly. "I have a booking here."

The clerk smiled. "Of course. I'll check. Your ID, please?"

Khadija hesitated. "I… I don't have my passport with me right now. My name is Khadija Ramzan. I'm from Pakistan."

The clerk tilted his head slightly. "Do you have a booking number or any other reference?"

She tried to steady her voice. "I've been here before—a while ago. Please just check my name. My uncle booked a room for me, for two years. He already paid the full amount in advance."

The clerk gave her a brief glance, then nodded. "Alright, I'll look. But I won't be able to give you a room without an ID."

He began typing. A few moments passed.

"Khadija Ramzan… from Pakistan?"

"Yes!" she said, a flicker of relief in her voice. Finally, something steady. A place to stay. A place to think.

But her relief was short-lived.

The clerk looked up and said flatly, “The booking was there—but it was a temporary hold. It was cancelled two days ago.”

Khadija froze.

“Cancelled? B-But why? Where will I go now?”

The words slipped from her lips in a whisper that trembled with fear.

Scene 60

The Clock Beneath the Ice

After days of scouring every lead, the police finally reached the secluded farm ranch. The place was silent—but not empty of signs. It was clear: Zafir had been there. But he and his captors were gone.

Meanwhile, after a gruelling three-day sea voyage, the icebreaker ship let them off deep in Hudson Bay. From there, the group took a smaller boat and reached Churchill—a remote Canadian town of just a thousand residents, known worldwide for its polar bears and beluga whales.

Tourists often came from far and wide to witness the icy beauty of the creatures.

But for Zafir, it was merely another cold prison.

They checked into a modest hotel for the night. Tomorrow, they would catch a flight to Winnipeg, then onward to Austin, Texas.

Zafir's mind raced.

Once I reach Austin, Professor Parker will realize I bluffed—he'll know I haven't made the progress I claimed.

And then what?

They might kill me. Which means… if I have any chance to change my fate—it has to be before we reach Austin.

Scene 61

The Sea Doesn't Shine the Same

Khadija stepped out of the hostel, suitcase in one hand, trolley bag in the other. She stood there on the street, overwhelmed and uncertain. Where could she go? What could she do now?

Across the road, she could see the Black Sea—the same sea that had looked breath-taking from her hotel terrace that morning. But now, under a shifting sky and a heavier heart, it felt different—ominous, even. Menacing in its stillness.

Today, she finally understood the meaning of the phrase:

"Beauty lies in the eyes of the beholder."

She glanced toward the sky with silent grief, as if asking heaven for an answer. Then, dragging her bags, she made her way to a nearby park.

There, she sat down and opened her suitcase, pulling out a few essential clothes to stuff into the trolley. She planned to abandon the larger bag—it was too heavy to drag around now.

While rummaging, her eyes fell on a book—one gifted to her by her friend Aamna on her birthday. She picked it up and stared at it, lost in thought. Then a thought sparked.

If I could just find internet somewhere... I remember Aamna's email address. Maybe I could contact her.

Trolley in tow, she stepped back onto the street, trying to summon courage and direction.

But the world still felt foreign.

She spotted a woman pushing a child in a stroller and hurried toward her, speaking in English. But the woman didn't understand. She smiled politely and walked on.

And just like that, the weight of her isolation grew heavier. Her heart began to race. The fear had arrived—cold, quiet, and very real.

Scene 62

Shadows Before Dawn

After landing in Winnipeg, it was already 7:00 p.m. Their flight to Austin wasn't until 5:00 the next morning. So they headed to a hotel near the airport.

Zafir was placed in a room with one of the men—his "handler," who was tasked with keeping watch. Given Zafir's apparent cooperation throughout their journey from Iqaluit, the guards had begun to relax their vigilance.

Zafir went to bed early.

The man remained up for a while, chain-smoking on the sofa... but fatigue crept up on him, and eventually he dozed off.

At 3:00 a.m., another team member entered the room, shaking him awake.

"Where's the boy?"

Confused and now fully alert, the man looked around the room—Zafir was gone.

Panic erupted.

The team leader stormed in, roaring with fury:

"Idiots! You were supposed to keep an eye on him—and you fell asleep? He slipped right through while you snored like donkeys!"

The guard, red with shame, muttered,

"He can't have gone far. His passport is still with us. We'll fan out across the area—he's got to be nearby."

But the boss wasn't having it. His voice thundered:

"Then go find him! And if you don't bring him back... don't bother coming back yourselves. Get moving!"

Scene 63

The Stranger with a Signal

It was evening as Khadija wheeled her trolley bag toward a nearby bus stop. A few people stood nearby, waiting. Moments later, a bus arrived. Several passengers boarded while one man stepped off and began walking away.

Khadija gathered her courage.

"Excuse me!" she called out.

The man stopped and turned, surprised. In Turkish, he asked,

"Did you say something to me?"

Khadija didn't understand him, so she asked:

"Do you speak English?"

The man responded in hesitant English,

"A little. Just... enough for help."

Khadija exhaled, relieved.

"I'm new here. I need to send an email. I don't have a phone or internet. Could you help me?"

The man looked at her, startled.

"You are tourist? And now... lost?"

Then, with a kind nod,

"Yes, I have internet. You can use my phone."

He handed her his phone. Khadija quickly composed an email to Aamna—brief, desperate. She explained her situation and pleaded, "Please go to Uncle Javed and tell him what I'm going through."

After sending it, she handed the phone back.

"Thank you so much."

The man smiled kindly.

"Welcome... goodbye."

He walked away.

And for the first time that day... something flickered in her heart.

Hope.

She believed that as soon as her elder uncle found out, he would help. But for now—where to go, where to rest... those questions still loomed like gathering clouds.

Scene 64

A Home on Borrowed Time

Winnipeg wasn't a foreign city for Zafir. He had spent part of his childhood there, and recently, his sister Saira had settled in after marrying Kashif, who worked for a multinational company.

After fleeing the hotel in the middle of the night, Zafir navigated the streets cautiously until dawn, finally arriving at a familiar doorstep. He rang the bell.

Saira opened the door—and froze in disbelief.

"Bhai jaan... you're here? Come in—please, come in!"

Zafir stepped inside. "How are you, Gudiya? How's Kashif?"

Beaming, she replied, "I'm great—and Kashif's fine too. He just left for work half an hour ago. But where have you been all these days? Mummy, Daddy—we were all so worried! And what's happened to you? You look awful!"

Zafir smiled faintly.

"So many questions, huh? At least let me eat something first—then I'll answer all of them."

Blushing a little, Saira said, "Sorry, Bhai jaan—I was so overwhelmed seeing you, I forgot. You freshen up, I'll make breakfast."

Zafir washed up and joined her in the kitchen. As she cooked, she asked, "Have you called Mummy or Daddy yet? They've been so scared for you."

His face dimmed. "No, Gudiya. And... I don't think I will. Not for now."

She paused. "What do you mean?"

Zafir lowered his voice, glancing toward the door.

"I've escaped from the custody of some extremely dangerous people. And I won't be staying here long. After breakfast, I'm leaving. I don't want anyone to know I was here. If anyone asks, I was never here. Understand?"

Saira placed the breakfast in front of him, concern written across her face.

"Oh Bhai jaan… that's terrifying. Okay. Let's talk through this. But first—eat."

Halfway through breakfast, Zafir said, "I need some money. Just enough to rent a place and stay hidden for a few days. Then I'll figure out my next move."

Saira nodded. "I only have a few hundred dollars at home, but I'll talk to Kashif and arrange more right away."

Zafir took a sip of tea.

"I don't feel great about taking money from your husband. But I don't have my ATM card anymore—and even if I did, I wouldn't use it. Those people have influence. They'll track me."

Saira asked, voice low, "What now, then?"

Zafir stared into the distance.

"I don't know. The whole world feels like a web of betrayal. The people you trust most… sometimes they're the first to stab you in the back. I don't even know who to believe anymore."

Her voice trembled as she murmured, "May Allah protect you."

Zafir turned to her, tone solemn.

"Listen carefully. Don't call Mummy or Daddy yet—nothing over the phone. Calls can be traced. Find a safe way to tell them I've escaped and that I'm hiding. They need to get my duplicate passport and ID sorted—because the originals are with those people. And tell Kashif, too… please be discreet. No one else must know."

Scene 65

Descent into Darkness

The sun had already set.

In small towns, evening silence falls heavy. It wasn't like the restless hum of big cities. Here, dusk arrived with a hush that clung to the walls and pressed against the heart. For Khadija, every breath felt heavier. The silence was so dense, it chilled the very blood in her veins.

She didn't know whether to scream or collapse in tears. Hunger gnawed at her. Her throat was parched.

Aimless, she began to walk. The road she was on was elevated. As she moved, it sloped gently downward, and from above, it appeared as though it poured directly into the sea—though in truth, it curved to meet another road that ran parallel to the Black Sea's edge.

As she descended, her trolley suddenly slipped from her hand and tumbled down. She rushed after it, but her foot caught on something—

She tripped, fell face-first onto the asphalt, and rolled—flailing, spiralling, down the slope.

A car appeared on the lower road. The driver saw it happen—saw the girl spinning out of control—and pulled over immediately. A family stepped out in alarm.

Khadija tried to rise, trembling, but her strength betrayed her. Blood trickled from her forehead, her elbows, her palms.

She took a step—then collapsed.

And this time... she did not get up.

Scene 66

The Scientist's Ultimatum

Professor Parker's voice crackled over the phone, edged with irritation.

"I'm a scientist, not a spy. You people should handle the boy's disappearance yourselves."

He paused, listening to the response on the other end. His voice lowered.

"Yes... he did mention once that his sister lives in Winnipeg. So it's possible—maybe even likely—that he's hiding there. That's all I can offer you on the matter."

He waited, then continued more calmly,

"I'm trying to begin work on the concept here with some capable students. But truthfully, Mr. Zafir had made significant progress already. If we had access to all of it, our job would be much easier. Starting from scratch... will be extremely difficult."

He exhaled.

"We don't even know the exact variables he used in his simulations and calculations. Without those, the entire model remains incomplete."

The voice on the other side spoke again, and Parker responded thoughtfully,

"I'll try, yes. But this is delicate, precision-based research. A single shift in parameters can ruin the entire result. The best solution is to find Mr. Zafir and send him to me. Once we have the basic modelling and initial calculations done, we won't need him anymore. After that... you can do with the boy whatever you wish."

Scene 67

A Voice Across Static

Zafir had checked into a cheap roadside motel. He lay low there for several days, gathering his thoughts and trying to remain invisible. Then one afternoon, disguised in a hat and sunglasses, he cautiously stepped outside.

At a nearby coin-operated public phone, he inserted a few coins and dialled.

After greeting his mother and assuring her he was okay, he asked softly,

"Is Daddy home?"

His mother's voice trembled with worry.

"Well, it's the weekend, so normally he would be. But today, Sheriff Peterson came over, and he left with him. My son, are you alright? Are you eating well? Is there any danger?"

Zafir gently reassured her.

"Don't worry, Mummy. I'm fine, Alhamdulillah. I just needed to speak to Daddy. I'll call again tonight at 8 p.m. Please tell him I need a new passport and ID as soon as possible. It's very difficult to move around without them. Alright… Khuda Hafiz."

Scene 68

No ID, No Name

Khadija's eyes fluttered open. She was lying on a hospital bed. A nurse stood beside her, scribbling something into a file.

Noticing that Khadija had regained consciousness, the nurse said something in Turkish—but Khadija didn't understand a word.

She tried to respond, but nothing made sense. The nurse simply gestured that she'd return shortly.

Khadija turned to glance at the clock on the wall.

2 o'clock.

But what kind of 2 o'clock? she thought.

It had been evening—maybe 7 or 8—when she'd fallen. Now it could be morning or the following afternoon.

She whispered to herself,

"Oh no… I've been unconscious for hours. But how did I even get here?"

Still caught in that haze of thought, she looked up to find the same nurse returning—with a doctor.

The doctor addressed her in English,

"We gave you a painkiller along with a sedative so you could rest."

Khadija nodded weakly,

"Thank you… but how did I get here?"

The doctor explained gently,

"An ambulance brought you in last night. Apparently, you collapsed on a road. Some passers-by called emergency services. We've treated your injuries. Now we'll need your ID or passport to complete your paperwork. And if you could clarify how you'll be paying?"

"Paying?" Khadija repeated in shock.

The doctor nodded,

"Yes. This is a private hospital. The paramedics assumed you were a tourist and brought you here. Local patients are usually treated at public hospitals for emergency care. If you have travel insurance, we'll verify its emergency coverage. Any balance will need to be settled in cash."

Khadija's voice trembled,

"Doctor… I have no ID, no passport… and no money."

"What?" the doctor said, stunned.

Khadija tried to clarify,

"I came here from Pakistan… to study. But I got… lost."

The doctor seemed baffled.

"Lost? I'm not sure I understand. But Miss—payment will be required. If you default, the hospital management may be forced to hand the matter over to the police."

Scene 69

A Farewell Between Shadows

A week had passed. Zafir sat in Central Library, his head tucked slightly beneath a hat, a book open before him. To any onlooker, he was just another reader absorbed in quiet study. But beneath the brim of that hat, his eyes watched every corner—waiting.

Minutes passed.

A girl in an abaya entered the library hall. Zafir subtly gestured with his hand. Instead of approaching directly, she made her way to a magazine stand, picked one up, and drifted casually toward his table. To the world, they were just two strangers buried in silent reading.

Without looking directly at him, Saira discreetly slid an envelope across the table. Zafir took it and slid it under his book.

Saira whispered,

"Bhai jaan, it has your Canadian passport, NICOP (ID Card for overseas Pakistani), a credit card—and ten thousand dollars. Daddy arranged everything."

Zafir nodded, softly.

"Gudiya, I'm going to miss you all so much."

Saira couldn't hold back her tears. Her voice cracked as she whispered,

"As soon as things calm down… please come back, Bhai jaan."

Zafir's face dimmed with sadness.

"I'm not going willingly, Gudiya. I'm only going because Daddy and the Sheriff thought it was safest. In-sha-Allah, I'll be back in a year... maybe sooner."

She blinked through her tears.

"You're going so far from all of us. May Allah protect you."

Zafir leaned closer, voice low.

"The U.S. or a major European country would've been too risky. That's why the Sheriff suggested Pakistan for now. Once things settle down, I'll either return quietly—or explore a safer option elsewhere."

Concern deepened in her voice.

"But Bhai jaan, you've never been to Pakistan. Where will you stay?"

Zafir gave a faint, guarded smile.

"Daddy has made arrangements. He has some friends in Islamabad—I'll stay with them at first. Then they'll help me settle."

Saira asked,

"When's your flight?"

"Tonight. First to Montreal, then Ankara. There's a 13-hour layover there. From Ankara, I'll fly to Islamabad. Long journey ahead," he replied.

Saira nodded, holding back another wave of emotion.

"May Allah carry you safely... and bring you safely back. Okay Bhai jaan—I should go. Kashif's waiting in the car."

Zafir said quietly,

"Okay, Gudiya. Allah Hafiz."

Scene 70

Missing Papers, Measured Words

Khadija flinched at the doctor's words. Suddenly, a thought struck her.

"My trolley bag… where is it?"

The doctor glanced at the nurse and exchanged a few words. She shook her head.

He turned to Khadija.

"Madam, the nurse who received you when the ambulance brought you in said there was no bag with you. Did your passport and money happen to be in it?"

Khadija hesitated.

If I say no, they might hand me over to Police. If I say yes—it's a lie…

Still unsure, she remained silent.

But the doctor continued on his own,

"You should file a police report about your missing trolley. That report will protect you from liability here and may also help the police recover your passport, money, and belongings."

Relieved at the way out, Khadija quickly said,

"Yes… I'll go to the police station and file a report."

The doctor nodded and turned to the nurse, giving her instructions. Then he looked back at Khadija, speaking more gently now:

"I've told the nurse to note on your discharge papers that you're a tourist and your bag, passport, and documents were lost. You'll be discharged in the morning—go straight to the police station from here."

Scene 71

The Door That Might Open

When Aamna unexpectedly received Khadija's email, she felt both surprise and warmth—touched that Khadija remembered her even from faraway Turkey. But that warmth quickly gave way to worry as she read through the desperate message.

Her heart racing, Aamna called Uncle Javed's home number.

His wife picked up, responding coldly,

"We don't know anything. She's probably fine there. I don't understand why you're so concerned."

Aamna tried to explain,

"But Aunty, she emailed me… she's in serious trouble—"

But the line went dead. She had hung up.

Now truly alarmed, Aamna didn't hesitate. She walked over to her parents' room and knocked lightly.

Her mother's voice came,

"Yes, Aamna dear, come in. Do you need something?"

Softly, Aamna replied,

"Yes, I need to talk to Baba."

Her father looked up.

"Of course, dear. What is it?"

Aamna handed over her phone, showing them Khadija's message and recounting everything.

He frowned thoughtfully.

"When you first told us your friend went to Turkey right after her intermediate exams, I found it odd. And now... this is serious. That poor girl is alone in a foreign land—struggling, probably terrified—and here, her family doesn't seem to care."

Aamna's mother added gently,

"Sometimes women in families can be narrow-minded, but men usually are more reasonable. I think we should speak to her uncle directly and let him know what's going on."

Her father nodded in agreement.

"Yes, that seems wise. Still, I can't believe how detached they're being. Don't worry, Aamna. I'll drive you to their house. You've met them before, right? I'll wait in the car. You go inside and talk to her uncle—tell him everything."

Scene 72

Waiting for a Signal

Morning air kissed her face as Khadija stepped out of the hospital. Relief washed over her—not from healing, but from escaping paperwork, questioning, and the looming threat of police reports.

Bandages still wrapped her head, hands, and one knee. Her body ached, but her mind churned faster.

Where is my trolley bag?

Her clothes—gone.

Her belongings—vanished.

The streets were quiet at this hour. The town, still nestled in a sleepy hush, paid her no mind. She wandered for a while, unsure where her feet were taking her, until one clear thought emerged:

I need to check my email. Maybe Aamna replied.

She spotted a girl riding by on a bicycle and waved her down with a hopeful gesture. The girl stopped, but didn't speak English. Just a confused smile and a shake of the head before riding on.

Khadija sighed and looked around.

If only I find someone who understands… maybe someone working in an office—someone who can help.

Eventually, she found herself sitting at a bus stand. The wooden bench felt oddly grounding. For now, it was a place to pause—a ledge between panic and patience.

And so she waited—not just for a bus, or for someone—but for a reply… a signal… anything that would mean she wasn't alone.

Scene 73

Shadows Beneath the Wings

Zafir landed in Ankara at 6 a.m. His connecting flight to Islamabad wasn't until 7 that evening—an agonizing thirteen-hour layover.

After clearing transit procedures, he settled into the lounge, ordered breakfast, and passed time browsing the internet. And then his eyes lit up.

"Wow… Aerospace and Aviation Museum?"

A grin tugged at his lips.

He checked the time—it was just past 7 a.m. The museum wouldn't open for another two hours. Still, he stood up, energized by the idea, and made his way to immigration.

Holding a Canadian passport, he was swiftly granted a transit visa. Moments later, he stepped out into the fresh Ankara air.

The sky was cloudless. The city stirred gently, unaware of the young man slipping past its edges.

Zafir hailed a taxi and directed it to the museum.

But what he didn't know was that behind him, in another part of the terminal, a pair of men watched.

They saw the cab pull away. And without wasting a second, they jumped into a nondescript car—and began the chase.

Scene 74

Truth That Stings

As Aamna and her father reached Khadija's uncle's house, he advised her gently:

"Beta, just deliver Khadija's message respectfully and come back. There's no need to argue or explain anything beyond that."

"Yes, Baba," Aamna nodded, and walked to the door.

Uncle Javed looked uncomfortable seeing her, and snapped,

"You already called Yasmin, my wife—and now you've come here yourself? What's your problem? Khadija is our responsibility and she's absolutely fine. You can leave."

Aamna wanted to say more—but remembered her father's words. She replied simply:

"Alright, Uncle. I'll go. Allah Hafiz."

She returned to the car with heavy steps.

Her father looked at her expectantly.

"What happened?"

"He scolded me and told me to leave. Said Khadija is fine," she answered glumly.

Her father thought for a moment, then said,

"Something doesn't feel right. Come on—I'll speak to them myself."

The house gate was open, so they stepped in quietly. Just as they reached the main door and were about to knock, they overheard Javed's harsh voice from inside:

"That cursed girl is sending emails again. Her friend just came over. What if the police show up tomorrow? I told them we should've used another way to get her property—but Bhai Sahib never listens to anyone."

Aamna and her father were stunned.

He signalled silently to his daughter,

"Let's go. Now."

They returned to the car and drove away, the weight of what they'd just heard sinking in.

Aamna was shaken.

"Baba... what was that? What are they even doing?"

Her father, deep in thought, said quietly:

"Beta, this is the world we live in. Not everyone is an angel—and not everyone is a devil either. But what's heart-breaking is how greed has blinded her relatives. They didn't even stop to think that she's a helpless orphan alone in a foreign land. Anything could happen to her. These people are just greedy and selfish."

Aamna asked, her voice tight with concern,

"But Baba—what will she do over there? She still thinks they just don't know what's going on."

Her father replied firmly:

"Then the first thing she needs is the truth. Even if it's painful, the truth must be told. Email her. Tell her exactly what we heard. She shouldn't be clinging to false hope. And tell her—if she needs money, we'll send whatever we can. But above all, she must contact the Pakistani embassy. In this situation, they're the only ones who can help her."

Aamna nodded, resolute.

"Yes, Baba. I'll do it right away."

Scene 75

The Stranger Who Stayed

Khadija had been sitting at the bus stop for some time when people gradually started appearing, the city finally stirring to life. She tried speaking to a few passers-by, but most didn't understand English or were simply in a rush.

Disheartened, she stood and began walking in a direction she chose blindly. Hunger gnawed at her. Her throat burned with thirst. She didn't know what to do… where to go.

She kept walking. When her body gave in, she'd rest on benches, watching strangers pass like waves. Eventually, she found herself near a mosque. It was already noon. Few had come for Zuhr prayer. As they left, she watched them silently and wandered inside, sinking onto a bench in the courtyard.

Soon, a man stepped out—an elderly gentleman, his beard thick with white. He noticed Khadija but at first didn't stop. Then he turned back.

In Turkish, he greeted and asked gently,

"Who are you? Why are you sitting here?"

Khadija didn't look up. Without returning the greeting, she said in English,

"I didn't understand a word you said."

The man smiled and repeated his question in English.

Khadija, drained and defensive, snapped,

"If my sitting here bothers you, I'll leave."

The man chuckled kindly.

"I have no problem with you sitting here. You're welcome to stay as long as you like. I only meant—if you're here for prayer, there's a women's section inside. It's shaded and cooler."

Khadija ignored the suggestion. Instead, she asked,

"Do you have a phone with internet?"

The man responded calmly,

"Yes, I do."

Khadija blurted,

"I need to check my email. Can I use your phone for a bit?"

He nodded and handed it over.

"Of course. No problem."

She took the phone and frantically opened her inbox.

And then—her breath caught.

Tears welled up and spilled without warning as she read Aamna's message. Her hands trembled. She couldn't bring herself to meet the man's eyes. Wordlessly, she extended the phone back to him.

Concerned, the man asked,

"Is everything alright? What happened?"

Sobbing, Khadija snapped,

"God has never done anything good for me. My fate is filled with disgrace, betrayal, and misery!"

The man didn't flinch at her outburst. He lowered his voice.

"Perhaps this isn't the moment to say otherwise… but please don't think like that. You're clearly hurting, deeply. You're injured… and alone. Let me ask—can I do anything to help you?"

Wiping her tears, Khadija whispered,

"Could I just have... some water?"

He nodded gently.

"Of course."

He stepped back into the mosque and returned moments later with a small bottle.

"Here. Drink," he said.

As she sipped, he added,

"My name is Jibran al-Jabrouni. I'm originally from a middle eastern country. Moved here years ago. I run a small business now. What's your name?"

"Khadija," she replied faintly.

"And how did you end up here... and with all these wounds?"

"I came to study from Pakistan," she said, her voice cracking.

"But now I'm wandering like a beggar."

Jibran nodded solemnly.

"If you're comfortable... there's a café just across the street. Let's go sit and talk. Maybe I can help."

Khadija, numb and drained after everything Aamna's email had revealed, simply nodded.

At the café, Jibran leaned forward and asked softly,

"Now tell me—what exactly is the trouble you're facing? Perhaps... I can be of some use."

Scene 76

Orders Without Borders

Inside the pursuing car, a phone rang.

A man picked up. A voice on the other end said,

"Looks like luck's finally on our side. We've got the chance to strike right here. Are you following him?"

The man answered,

"Yes, we're on him."

The voice on the line cautioned,

"Make sure it's done without alerting Turkish police or drawing public attention. Understood?"

As he toyed with a pistol in his lap, the man replied with a sneer,

"That's child's play for us. We'll wrap this up soon and send you some good news."

But the voice on the line repeated, firmer now:

"I'm saying it again—be careful. We don't have any understanding with the authorities here. Back in Pakistan, we had police and certain officials on our side. The plan was to finish him off as soon as he stepped out of the airport. But now that we have the opportunity here in Turkey... why wait any longer?"

Scene 77

The First Step Toward Somewhere

After listening to Khadija's entire story, Jibran al-Jabrouni leaned back and said,

"So that's the situation. In these circumstances, your first step should be reporting to your embassy and getting your documents reissued. And I understand—you probably don't want to go anywhere near those people again."

Khadija replied with uncertainty in her voice:

"I don't even know where the embassy is… or how I'd get there. And if I don't go back, then where else would I go?"

Jibran thought for a moment.

"Most embassies are in Ankara—it's the capital. But it's far from here. A little over an hour by flight. I'll take you myself. As for whether you go back to Pakistan or consider another option—we'll talk about that later."

Khadija looked at him, her eyes wary.

"Why are you doing all this… for me?"

He replied gently,

"From the way you speak, I can tell—your pain wasn't caused by strangers. It came from those who should've protected you. So let me just say this: don't worry. If you're comfortable, you can stay at my home tonight—or I can book you a hotel room. Tomorrow morning, we'll fly to Ankara. Straight to your embassy."

Khadija, still fragile but grateful, whispered:

"Thank you. Please… book me into a hotel."

Scene 78

Trap at the Museum Gate

Zafir stepped out of the taxi, paid the driver, and dismissed him with a nod. A mild morning breeze tousled his hair as he slung a small satchel over his shoulder and walked toward the entrance of the Aerospace & Aviation Museum. A security checkpoint stood just outside the sleek glass doors. He presented his ID casually, exchanged a smile with the bored guard, and disappeared inside—unaware of the shadows trailing him.

Across the street, a nondescript black sedan had been parked for nearly ten minutes. Inside it sat three men, dressed plainly but sharp-eyed. One of them put down a pair of binoculars and murmured into a phone:

"He's entered the museum. Target's isolated."

He ended the call and turned to the man in the back seat, who was quietly assembling a compact silenced weapon.

The driver—bearded, calm, methodical—asked,

"What's the plan once he's out?"

The man in the back replied,

"We keep a taxi on standby near the exit. When he comes out, our guy pretends to be a driver offering a ride. He gets in, and we take him off the grid. No noise. No struggle."

The driver nodded, eyes still on the side mirror.

"And we follow that taxi in another SUV. Clean handoff. We finish the job quickly, then vanish."

The third man, still watching the entrance, added coldly,

"Just remember—we can't afford mistakes here. There's no backup. No friendly cops. Here, one wrong move and we'll be hunted ourselves."

The man with the gun smirked,

"Relax. It's a public museum. Too easy. Once he's isolated on the way out, the rest is routine."

All three men sat in silence as a tour bus pulled up, momentarily blocking their view. Zafir, now inside, wandered between exhibits—marvelling at scaled fighter jets and vintage gliders. He was at ease. Even inspired.

But outside, a web was tightening—one thread at a time.

Scene 79

The Mask Falls

After submitting her request at the Pakistani Embassy in Ankara for a duplicate passport, Khadija and Jibran al-Jabrouni stepped outside. She turned to him and said,

“Thank you so much for helping me like this. I don’t know how I can ever repay you.”

He opened the car door for her with a smile.

“Come, sit. We can talk on the way.”

Jibran had rented a car from Ankara Airport. As they drove toward the hotel, he spoke with a tone meant to sound casual:

“My wife passed away several years ago. My children are grown and absorbed in their own lives… I live alone in Trabzon now.”

Something about the shift made Khadija uneasy. Why was he telling her all this?

Then, with an air of gentle insistence, he continued,

“I’m a bit older than you, but I need a sincere partner to share my loneliness. And you… you’re hurting, alone—you need someone strong to lean on too.”

Khadija frowned, unsettled.

“W-What do you mean by that?”

And then he said it, plainly:

“I want to marry you.”

"What! What are you saying?" she gasped, shocked and furious.

He remained calm.

"There's nothing wrong with it religiously. I need a companion—you need support. It's a win-win deal."

Khadija's voice sharpened.

"So this was the price for your kindness?"

Jibran didn't even flinch.

"Even if I thought of it that way—is that wrong? Given your situation, marriage to me would solve everything."

Rage surged in her voice.

"I refuse. Let me out right now. I don't need your help anymore."

Then, casually but deliberately, he placed a hand on hers. She yanked it away and shouted:

"What do you think you're doing? Stop the car—now!"

He sighed.

"Why are you being stubborn? This is for your own good."

Her voice cut like a blade:

"Stop the car—or I'll open the door and jump out while it's moving!"

Startled, he quickly blurted,

"Alright, alright. Just calm down and shut the door—I'll stop up ahead."

Khadija slammed the door shut. A flurry of honking erupted from nearby cars, startled by the sudden opening mid-traffic. Passers-by began to glance their way in confusion.

Jibran eased the car to the side of a quieter stretch of road.

And then, as he slowed, he reached toward her again—but before he could touch her, she threw the door open and bolted from the car.

Jibran shouted after her and jumped out, giving chase.

Scene 80

Mirror Signals and Split-Second Decisions

The museum wasn't quite what Zafir had expected. There weren't any scientific exhibits as he had hoped—just scale models of old aircraft, aviation history displays, and a range of aviation memorabilia. It was charming in its own right, just not the immersive technological dive he had imagined.

Still, he spent nearly two hours exploring every gallery before finally stepping out into the warm Ankara afternoon. As he glanced around for a ride, a taxi pulled up beside him.

The driver leaned out and asked in English,

"Where to?"

Zafir replied,

"Airport."

The driver nodded.

"150 lira."

"Alright. Let's go," Zafir agreed and slid into the backseat.

The taxi pulled away smoothly.

A black SUV, parked discreetly nearby, started its engine and began to follow.

Inside the SUV, a man made a call.

"He's in our taxi. The driver's taking him to the location we told him. Our guys are already stationed there. I'm trailing behind. You'll hear good news soon."

Zafir gazed out the window, watching the city roll past. But something made him glance up—perhaps it was instinct, perhaps just the flicker of unease. The driver was peeking at him again and again through the rear-view mirror.

At first, Zafir brushed it off. But then he realized—the driver wasn't looking at him. He was eyeing the rear-view, checking a vehicle behind them repeatedly.

Zafir subtly turned to glance behind. A black SUV tailed them relentlessly—too close, too focused.

Something wasn't right.

He looked at the driver again. Far from appearing nervous, the man seemed composed... even satisfied.

Zafir narrowed his eyes.

"Is there a problem? You keep looking behind us," he asked calmly.

The driver flinched.

"No, nothing. Everything is fine," he muttered.

Zafir scanned the surroundings, then said firmly,

"I'm not from this city, but I have a sharp memory. This isn't the route we took from the airport to the museum."

The driver faltered,

"This is... an alternate way. A shortcut."

And that was it—confirmation.

Zafir turned again. The black SUV still followed, unwavering. It wasn't paranoia anymore.

As soon as the taxi slowed at a red light, Zafir made his move.

He flung the door open and sprinted into a side alley—vanishing before the driver could stop him.

Behind him, the SUV screeched to a halt. The doors flew open. Several armed men poured out and began chasing him down the narrow lane.

Scene 81

Crossroads of Fate

Zafir was sprinting at full speed, heart pounding like a war drum, when he turned sharply into a narrow alley. His lungs burned, but his legs didn't stop. The alley ended—he rounded the corner blindly.

And then—

Crash!

He collided head-on with a girl charging in from the opposite direction. Both were hurled to the ground with a brutal thud. Heads hit asphalt. Shock flared first, then pain.

It was Khadija.

They sat upright, holding their heads, breathless from impact.

"I'm so sorry," Zafir gasped. "I didn't see you—I was being chased—"

"I'm sorry too," Khadija whispered, wincing. "I was running away from someone too... didn't see you..."

From behind Zafir came the stomp of boots—shouts closing in.

Far behind Khadija, Jibran al-Jabrouni emerged into view, scanning frantically.

Zafir staggered to his feet.

"They're here. They are after me." He worriedly said.

Khadija pointed shakily to the other side.

"The man chasing me... he's coming from over there."

No further questions. No hesitation.

Zafir extended a hand. “Come on.”

Khadija grabbed it. He pulled her to her feet.

“Run.” Zafir shouted.

And they did.

Side by side. Strangers by fate, but now tethered by danger.

Behind them, two dangers approached from opposite ends—Jibran from one, armed men from the other. And in the middle, Zafir and Khadija fled into the unknown, lungs burning, limbs aching, but a strange flicker of hope sparking between each footfall.

Scene 82

Pedals and Pulse beats

They had run far—faster and longer than either of them thought they could—but now Khadija came to a stumbling halt. Her chest heaved, breath ragged and sharp. Zafir, a few paces ahead, stopped and turned back.

"What's wrong?" he asked, trying to keep his own breath steady.

Khadija bent slightly, clutching her ribs. Her words came out broken between gasps:

"Can't… can't run anymore… my legs… they're in so much pain…"

Zafir looked behind, scanning the alley for movement. Then, glancing side to side, he murmured with a wry twist of his lips:

"Looks like I'll have to commit a sin… to survive."

Khadija blinked through the sweat on her brow.

"W-What do you mean?"

Zafir gave a half-smile that didn't reach his eyes.

"We need to steal. Stay here. I'll be back."

He darted off toward a nearby house. In its porch stood a simple bicycle—unguarded.

Moments later, he raced back toward her, pedalling fast.

"There's no better option right now. Will you get on?"

Khadija hesitated.

But shouts echoed behind them—boots on stone.

Zafir turned, panicked.

"Please tell me—quick—because I'll have to go. I think if they see me, they'll shoot."

Khadija slid forward onto the front bar of the bike, curling in tight.

Without another word, Zafir began to pedal.

Hard.

The roads in this district of Ankara weren't kind. Slopes. Dips. Steep cuts through hillocks. But they pushed forward, gritting through the pain in their legs and lungs.

Eventually, Zafir's pace slowed to a manageable rhythm. His ankles ached from the strain, and sweat trickled down his neck.

"I think we've left them far behind. This road leads to some kind of countryside. Fields, I think."

Khadija, equally sore from sitting hunched over, whispered:

"Let's stop. Just for a bit."

He pulled to the side. She climbed down. Zafir leaned the bike against a tree, then collapsed into the grass, stretching his cramping legs.

Khadija stood a few steps away, glancing back down the road—the way they'd come.

Eyes sharp.

Breath still unsure.

And fate... still uncertain.

Scene 83

A Mother's Voice Denied

“What do you mean, Javed bhai, you haven’t been in contact with Khadija? Please, give me her phone number. I’ll call and check on her myself,” Arifa asked, her voice tight with worry.

Javed snapped,

“And by what right are you asking me these questions? You were the one who chose to leave Ramzan bhai. So why are you calling me now?”

Arifa’s voice trembled,

“I’m not calling because of the past—I’m calling because of my daughter. Your niece. I haven’t heard from her in days. Is she alright in Turkey?”

Javed replied with biting sarcasm,

“Forgive me, but if you truly cared so much about her, you wouldn’t have left her behind all those years ago to be raised by others while you lived your life in peace. Anyway, she’s absolutely fine. She lives in a beautiful hostel and studies at one of the best private universities there.”

Relieved but still uneasy, Arifa said,

“Oh, thank God she’s okay. But her phone’s been unreachable. If you have another number for her, please share it. Hearing her voice would ease my heart.”

Javed, spinning a lie with ease, replied,

“Liaqat speaks to her daily. She has a local number there, but she explicitly told us not to share it with anyone, especially you. So please—don’t call here again.”

Scene 84

A World Made of Lies

Zafir lay on the grass, eyes scanning the open sky above, and murmured,

"I've heard it said many times—this world is full of deception. But it's only recently that I've truly experienced how everyone you meet... can betray you. Anyway—who were you running from?"

Khadija stood with her back to him, still watching the road behind.

Without turning, she said quietly,

"An old man who tried to buy my gratitude by demanding marriage as compensation. When I refused, he got aggressive... so I ran."

Zafir, still lost in his own storm, replied,

"I see... I put blind faith in a professor. He used me. Betrayed me. Sent professional killers after me—the same ones who made me run for my life."

Khadija added, her voice raw,

"I trusted my uncle and his family. Turns out, they threw me to the wolves. Left me to suffer and die in a land not my own."

Zafir shot back almost immediately,

"Exactly! This is what I meant. This world is a mirage—and most people offer only betrayal. In my case, it came from strangers. In yours... from your own.

By the way, I'm Zafir Suhban. From Iqaluit, Canada."

Khadija replied,

"Khadija Ramzan... I have no home. And I—"

Her sentence cut off.

Alarmed, she snapped her head around.

"Get up—quick! A car's heading this way—fast!"

Zafir leapt to his feet and saw the speeding vehicle.

"We can't outrun them on the bike," he said.

"This looks like farmland—those are olive trees. Let's cut through the fields. I don't know if they're after you or me—but either way, this is our best chance."

Without another word, they darted into the olive grove, weaving through the gnarled trees as branches swayed gently above them.

Somewhere behind... wheels crunched gravel.

But ahead—there was still room to run.

Scene 85

No Loose Ends

"Well, that's done," Khadija's uncle said with satisfaction.

"All the property has been sold, and the money's been transferred into our accounts. Even the funds stuck in Ramzan's account were released by the bank."

His younger brother, Liaqat, nodded in agreement.

"Yes, bhai jaan. Everything's gone smoothly. The shares have landed safely into our respective bank accounts."

But Javed seemed uneasy.

"That may be so, but there are two remaining issues. First, the girl Khadija emailed—her friend. If she creates trouble or goes to the police, things could get very complicated for us."

The elder brother waved off the concern,

"Don't stress. What connection does that girl really have with Khadija? Let her shout all she wants—she'll lose her voice and settle down soon enough."

"Forget her. What's the second issue?"

Javed's voice dropped into a more troubled tone.

"Arifa called—from Sharjah. She was very anxious. Asked for Khadija's number. For now, I managed to shut it down, but we'll need a solid story soon—one that permanently buries this entire matter."

Scene 86

A Call That Reconnects

Zafir and Khadija had walked deep through the olive fields before collapsing again onto the earth, exhausted.

Zafir said,

“They won’t find us here. Let’s wait until dusk… then we head back.”

Khadija nodded, and just then Zafir checked his watch.

“Oh my God !!! ” he exclaimed.

Startled, Khadija turned.

“W-What happened?”

Zafir rubbed his hands over his face.

“I had a flight to Islamabad this evening. There’s no way I’ll catch it now.”

Khadija gasped,

“You’re going to Islamabad too?”

He looked at her, surprised.

“Are you?”

Her voice faltered.

“I… I don’t know.”

“You don’t know?” Zafir asked, puzzled.

She didn’t answer right away. Then she asked,

"Do you have a phone with internet?"

"I do," he said. "But I doubt there's signal here. Let me check."

He looked at his phone.

"Yeah, no coverage here. We'll try again as we head back. But... why do you need it?"

Khadija replied,

"I'm waiting for an email. From a friend."

Zafir glanced toward the horizon.

"The sun's down. It's getting dark fast. I doubt they're still out looking for us. Let's get moving."

Khadija agreed. They retraced their steps to the road—relieved to find their bicycle untouched where they'd left it.

"Thank God," Zafir said. "Let's ride to the city. I'll find a taxi from there to the airport. What about you?"

"I just want to check my email," she murmured.

Once inside city limits, Zafir abandoned the bicycle by a wall and said,

"Let's walk from here. We'll find a taxi up ahead."

Khadija followed.

"Can you check your phone now? Maybe we've got signal."

Zafir checked.

"Ah—full bars! Here, check your email."

Khadija had asked Aamna in her last message to contact her mother's family in Rawalpindi and somehow get her mother's number.

And now—there it was.

Aamna's reply said she had visited Khadija's maternal relatives with her father. After a long struggle, they had finally given her Arifa's number.

Khadija lit up.

"Can I call Sharjah using your phone?"

Zafir nodded.

"Of course."

Khadija dialled. As soon as the call connected, Arifa answered anxiously,

"My child! Are you alright? I kept calling your uncle, asking for your number, but he never gave it. Thank God you called. How are you?"

With emotion trembling in her voice, Khadija said,

"I need to tell you something..."

"Yes, my dear—go on."

She told her mother everything in brief.

Arifa's voice turned sharp with anger.

"I knew it. That's why they were dodging my questions and piling on lies."

Then Khadija gathered her courage.

"I... need to ask something else."

"Go ahead, my child," Arifa urged.

A deep breath.

"Can I... come live with you?"

Arifa's voice broke slightly.

"Of course! You have no safe place now… I'll talk to Nasir and call you back on this number."

When the call ended, Khadija handed the phone back.

"Thank you. Can we wait here a little? My mother's going to call again."

Zafir smiled softly.

"No worries. Keep the phone with you. Sit tight—I'll go grab something to drink. My throat feels like sandpaper."

Scene 87

Between a Tear and a Prayer

Zafir returned with some food from the nearby shop, only to find Khadija still on the phone—tears streaming down her face.

"You're still helpless... even now?" she sobbed.

"My mother's side has rejected me, my father's side deceived me, my stepfather can't stand my existence, and you—my own mother—can do nothing for me. Where am I supposed to go?"

On the other end, Arifa's voice was trembling too.

"I begged Nasir, pleaded with him... but he didn't budge. He even gave me an ultimatum: choose between him and you. My child, somehow... somehow just return to Pakistan and go to your maternal uncle. I'll call him. He'll take you in."

Khadija's voice cracked.

"If even a mother can't help, then what hope is left from the world? I'm ashamed I begged for your help—pushed down my pride for this."

She took a breath, then added coldly,

"I'll never call you again."

She hung up and clutched her face in both hands, sobbing uncontollably.

From a short distance, Zafir had witnessed it all. He stepped away quietly, giving her a few minutes of space.

When he returned, she had composed herself—dried her tears, rebuilt the mask.

He approached gently, handed her the bottle and snacks.

"Sorry I took a while… here, this is for you."

Khadija accepted them, murmuring,

"Thank you." She handed back his phone.

Zafir tucked it into his pocket.

"Eat and drink a bit. I'll just offer my prayer over there, by the tree. Lost a few too many these past few days running from devils. In the meantime, you eat in peace."

He poured water from a bottle to make wudu, then opened his phone to find the Qibla direction.

As he stood in stillness, folding his arms in prayer beside the tree, Khadija sat cross-legged nearby… quietly drinking, eating, and recovering from the ache of a door she'd hoped might open… and watching another person kneel to speak with something far beyond both of them.

Scene 88

Help Offered, Dignity Kept

As Zafir finished his prayer, Khadija had already eaten and was sitting quietly. He asked,

"So… what's the plan now?"

Before she could reply, his phone rang.

Khadija's expression tensed.

"It's probably my mother. Please don't answer. I don't want to speak with her anymore. Just block the number."

Zafir replied gently,

"Let me see who it is first."

He checked the screen. His face brightened.

"Assalam-o-alaikum! Gudiya, how are you?"

Saira's cheerful voice came through:

"I'm good, Bhai jaan. And Kashif too! You must be waiting for boarding to start..."

"Not yet," Zafir said. "Something came up, and I missed my flight. Still in Ankara. I'll try to get on the next one."

Saira sounded concerned.

"What happened? Are you okay?"

"Yeah, I'm fine. I'll explain everything later. Just let Mummy and Daddy know. And tell Daddy to inform his friend in Islamabad that I'll be arriving late. I texted him, but he might not have seen it yet."

"Got it, Bhai jaan. I'll call him now. Just let me know when you land. Take care. Allah Hafiz."

Zafir ended the call and smiled.

"That was Saira—my younger sister. She lives in Winnipeg with her husband."

Khadija simply nodded.

"So… what will you do now?" he asked. "I'm heading to the airport to catch another flight."

Khadija replied softly,

"The embassy asked me to come back in two days for my new passport."

Zafir thought for a moment.

"Ah, so you've got to wait here then?"

She didn't answer—just turned her face away. Her eyes shimmered again.

"I'll stay here until I get my passport. You go ahead."

Zafir hesitated.

"Alright then… I should get going."

He took a step, but her voice stopped him.

"Wait…"

He turned quickly.

"Yes?"

After a deep breath, she asked,

"Could you… could you help me, just a little more?"

Zafir gave a sheepish smile.

"Honestly, I didn't want to leave you like this anyway. But I held back in case you'd take offense if I offered unsolicited help. Tell me—what do you need? If I can, I will help."

She hesitated.

"Could you… maybe help me book a hotel for two nights? Just until I get my passport and return to Pakistan?"

Zafir nodded.

"Of course. That's not a problem at all. Come with me."

He hailed a taxi, and they reached a nearby hotel. Zafir booked a room for four nights—just to be safe—and paid for both the room and meals in advance. Handing Khadija the key card, he said:

"Room 1205, on the twelfth floor. You go ahead. I'll head to the airport now."

Khadija's voice was full of quiet gratitude:

"Thank you. If life ever gives me the chance, I'll repay this kindness."

Zafir responded softly,

"Okay… and here—take this money. It'll help with your ticket and other expenses. I really have to go now. Assalam-o-alaikum."

Taking the money, Khadija replied,

"Thank you."

Zafir paused, turned with a smile and said playfully,

"'Thank you' isn't the correct reply to Assalam-o-alaikum. It's Wa alaikum assalam.

Assalam-o-alaikum."

Khadija finally smiled, even through her tears.

"Wa alaikum assalam."

Scene 89

A Place to Disappear

When Zafir landed in Islamabad, his father's friend, Babar Durrani, was waiting at the airport to receive him. They drove together through the city and eventually reached Babar's home.

After dinner, as tea was being served, Babar said warmly,

"Beta, you're most welcome to stay with us. But Farooq mentioned you'd be staying in Islamabad for a year or two. So I've rented a fully furnished two-bedroom apartment for you in F-8. Here's the key. You're welcome to spend the night here and move in tomorrow."

Zafir took the key with gratitude.

"Thank you so much, Uncle. I'll stay here tonight and move in the morning. Actually… I'll also need to rent a car."

Uncle nodded.

"No problem. I'll have one arranged by morning. But just a heads-up—cars here are right-hand drive. Think you'll manage alright?"

Zafir smiled.

"In Iqaluit, cars are rare. But yeah—in bigger cities people drive left-hand and struggle to adjust here. I should be fine though, In sha'Allah."

Babar Durrani smiled approvingly.

"Alright then, beta. You rest now. You've had a long journey."

Scene 90

Echoes Between Strangers

The next day, Zafir moved into his new apartment. It was spacious and comfortable. He made himself a cup of coffee and sat down with his laptop.

Just then, his phone rang.

The number was unfamiliar.

He hesitated—then ignored it.

Moments later, it rang again. Same number. This time, Zafir checked the country code.

Sharjah.

It clicked. This had to be the number Khadija had used to call her mother. After a moment of reflection, he picked up.

A frantic voice burst through:

"Oh, my child! Thank God you answered. I've been so worried. I called your uncle—he says your maternal uncle will take you in. Why won't you say anything?"

Zafir spoke gently.

"I believe… you're Khadija's mother?"

There was confusion on the other end.

"W-Who are you? Where's Khadija?"

"My name is Zafir. In Ankara, Khadija borrowed my phone to call you."

Her voice cracked with rising panic.

"Oh—where is she? Can I speak to her?"

Zafir replied calmly,

"She's still in Ankara. Her passport was lost, so the embassy gave her a two-day window to collect the duplicate."

There was a pause—then worry returned with urgency.

"Who are you? And how do you know my daughter?"

Zafir answered plainly,

"By chance. We crossed paths through an unfortunate accident. We were together briefly. I've since travelled to Islamabad. She stayed behind."

Arifa's voice trembled,

"Do you know where she is? Which hotel?"

Zafir spoke gently,

"Please don't worry. She's in a hotel, safe. She'll only be able to travel once she receives her passport."

Desperate now, Arifa said,

"Do you have her number? I just want to hear my daughter's voice again."

Zafir paused, thinking, then replied,

"Give me a little time. I'll try to find a way to get you in touch."

Her voice broke again,

"You'd bring peace to a mother's heart. You'll have my endless prayers. Please… just once… let me speak to her."

Zafir responded softly,

"I'll try, Aunty. I'll let you know. Assalam- o-alaikum."

Scene 91

Held Between Two Silences

Zafir returned to his laptop, jotting down a phone number on a notepad. He glanced at the time and murmured,

"It must be morning over there by now... let's try."

He dialled the number for the hotel where Khadija was staying.

"Please connect me to Room 1205," he requested at reception.

When the call connected, he said cheerfully,

"Assalam-o-alaikum."

A surprised voice responded,

"Yes? Who's this?"

Zafir chuckled softly,

"That's not how you reply to Assalam-o- alaikum, you know. The proper answer is Wa alaikum assalam. Let's try again—Assalam-o-alaikum."

Khadija recognized the voice and blinked, startled.

"Oh—it's you!"

Zafir smiled.

"Yep, it's me. Still waiting on the proper reply though."

She replied quietly,

"Wa alaikum assalam... I thought you'd left for Pakistan?"

"I did," he said. "Calling from Islamabad, actually. Are you alright?"

Khadija, still puzzled, asked,

"You called from Islamabad… just to check on me?"

Zafir corrected gently,

"Not exactly. Your mother called my phone earlier—she was very worried and wanted to speak with you."

Khadija's tone cooled.

"But I don't want to speak with her."

Zafir paused a moment.

"Alright. I'll pass that message along. It's between you and her, and it's not my place to step in."

Then softly,

"Okay, I'll hang up now. Take care."

He ended the call.

Then leaned back in his chair.

And let silence do what silence does best: hold everything that can't yet be said.

Scene 92

Shutting Down Shadows

Professor Parker spoke into the phone, his tone weary yet resolute:

"I've been working on this for the past week. I even got my best students and fellow professors involved. Honestly, I think the progress Mr. Zafir claimed to have made was completely unfounded."

A voice on the other end responded coldly:

"So he lied just to save his skin… made bold claims, deceived us, and slipped away. And it worked."

Professor Parker nodded grimly.

"That's exactly what it looks like. His research proposal sounded exciting, yes—but practically? I don't believe it's viable at all."

The voice on the line fell silent for a beat. Then firmly stated:

"Fine. I'll notify my boss—there's no point in pursuing this. Shut it down."

Scene 93

A Place She Might Still Belong

An hour later, Zafir dialled Arifa's number. After greeting her, he spoke with gentle clarity:

"Aunty, I called your daughter at the hotel where she's staying. I did speak to her... but I'm sorry—she doesn't wish to talk to you right now."

He heard her breath falter—and then tears.

"She's very angry with me... and honestly, she has every right to be," Arifa whispered. "But she's still my child—my heart. How can I sit here while she's left alone like this?"

Her voice broke.

"Son, if she picks up your call again, can I ask you to do me one favour—please?"

Zafir responded quietly,

"Of course, Aunty. What is it?"

Arifa steadied herself.

"She doesn't want to stay with her uncles—her mother's family. And for certain reasons, I can't bring her here to Sharjah. But I spoke to an old friend of mine, Zarina Baloch, from my school days. She lives in Rawalpindi with her husband and two daughters—they're Khadija's age. She's willing to take Khadija in."

"I'll send you her address and phone number. Please... pass it to Khadija. Let her know she has somewhere safe—somewhere she won't feel so unwanted."

Zafir paused for a moment, thinking, then said softly:

“Alright, Aunty. I’ll call her and share your message.”

Scene 94

A Message, Despite Everything

The next morning, Zafir glanced at the time and figured Khadija might be awake. He dialled the hotel reception and asked to be connected to Room 1205.

"Assalam-o-alaikum. How are you?" he said once the line connected.

Khadija's tone was flat.

"Wa alaikum assalam. I'm fine. Why are you calling?"

Zafir asked gently,

"Did you get your passport yesterday?"

"Yes," she replied. "And I've also bought my return ticket to Pakistan."

Zafir brightened.

"That's great news. When's your flight?"

"Tonight," she said. "I'll land in Islamabad at 5 a.m."

Zafir hesitated, then added carefully,

"I hope you don't mind, but your mother called again. She's really worried. May I pass on a message from her?"

Khadija's voice sharpened:

"I don't want to talk to her, or hear anything she has to say. Have you become her messenger now?"

Zafir couldn't help smiling at her bluntness.

"Wow—well said. But no, not exactly. It's just that whenever she calls, it reminds me of my own mummy. That's all.

But if you'll allow it, please just hear her message. Do whatever you like afterward."

Khadija thought for a moment. Then quietly,

"Alright. Go ahead—what did she say?"

Zafir relayed Arifa's message carefully, passing along the contact number and address of Zarina Baloch in Rawalpindi—the friend who had agreed to take Khadija in.

Once she had noted it down, the call ended. No goodbyes. Just an understanding, hovering quietly at the edge of silence.

Scene 95

Crossed Wires, Unspoken Truths

That evening, Zafir called Arifa again and shared the update. He had spoken to Khadija and relayed the information about Zarina Baloch.

Arifa's voice trembled with gratitude.

"Beta, may Allah make you the coolness of your parents' eyes and grant you every joy in this life and the next. That's the prayer of a broken mother."

Zafir replied softly,

"Ameen. Aunty... if you don't mind, can I say something?"

"Of course, beta." She said.

He hesitated, choosing his words carefully.

"I don't think your daughter is going to go to that woman's house."

Arifa was startled.

"W-Why not? She has no other place. Her paternal relatives destroyed her. And she won't go to her maternal family either. Zarina is the only safe place left—she should go."

Zafir answered gently,

"I don't fully understand family politics. I was raised in Iqaluit, Canada—just me, my parents, my little brothers and a sister. That was our whole world. But... I do get the sense your daughter has been through something so deeply unfair, it's turned her rebellious... distant from faith even. I'm sorry to say it bluntly."

Arifa sighed, a long cold breath.

"You're probably right. When her grandmother was alive, Khadija stayed with her. She was more grounded then. But after everything her uncles did… she's completely lost faith in people.

Even I… her mother… she won't speak to me. If she doesn't go to Zarina, how will I ever find her in this world? At least, right now, you're my only link to her."

Zafir, caught in his own storm, said quietly,

"I wish I could say more, Aunty. I'm just dealing with my own mess—barely escaped with my life from Canada and hiding out here in Islamabad in complete anonymity."

This startled Arifa.

"W-What do you mean? Did you commit a crime? Who's after you?"

Zafir smiled faintly.

"No crime, Aunty. I was passionate about research and fell in with dangerous, deceptive people. Just barely managed to get out. My family back home is worried. But thank God, I'm safe now. My dad's old friend—Babar Durrani—helped me find a place here."

Arifa froze.

"BB... Babar… Durrani? The one who lives in F-6 Islamabad?"

"Yes, Aunty. You know him?" Zafir's voice lifted with surprise.

But Arifa didn't respond right away. She couldn't bring herself to say it. That this Babar Durrani was none other than the elder brother of her ex-husband Ramzan. That he—this same man—was one of those responsible for Khadija's downfall, the one who shipped her off to Turkey and left her to fend for herself.

She stayed quiet.

"Aunty? Everything alright? You've gone silent. It's okay. I know you're probably just worried about your daughter. I'll be here if you need anything. Allah Hafiz."

Zafir ended the call and returned to his laptop.

But Arifa sat in paralyzed thought.

Should she tell him? Should she pull this thread?

Or should she stay silent—because right now, her only real fear was Khadija's pride pushing her over an edge she might never come back from. If she didn't go to Zarina... where in this wide world would Arifa ever find her daughter again?

Scene 96

Missed Meetings and Quiet Warnings

Zafir had ordered several books online, determined to turn time into something useful. In his apartment, he kept entirely to himself—no conversations with neighbours, no exposure. He offered 'Isha prayer at a nearby mosque and, after returning, sat down with a book. Just as he was about to sleep, his phone rang.

The number was unfamiliar.

He hesitated, then answered.

"Hello?"

A familiar voice teased,

"No Assalam-o-Alaikum today?"

He smiled.

"Oh! It's you. Wa Alaikum Assalam. What number is this? It looked strange—I honestly got nervous."

Khadija replied,

"Worried it might be one of those men still after you?"

Zafir murmured,

"Exactly that. But you're in a much better mood than usual. What prompted this call?"

"I'm at the airport, in the departure lounge. There's a coin-operated phone here, so I thought I'd call.

And yes, I'm a little more at ease today. One friend—perhaps my only friend—has arranged a place for me. Her family rents out the upper floor of their home, and it's currently vacant. She promised to let me stay there for a few months."

"That's good news," Zafir said. "Although, had you accepted your mother's offer and gone to her friend's place, it might've been better. I'm sure your mother wouldn't choose something that could harm you."

But Khadija interjected quickly,

"Let's skip that. Do you have a local Pakistani number? This seems like your Canadian one."

Zafir, surprised, said,

"Actually, yes—I just got one today. But why do you ask?"

Her tone grew restrained.

"I want to return the money you gave me. I don't want to carry that favour. I won't be able to do it immediately, but I'll try to return it as soon as I can."

He gave her the number. Then, cautiously:

"If your mother calls me again, should I tell her anything?"

Khadija began,

"No need to tell her—"

But the line disconnected mid-sentence.

Zafir stared at the phone and muttered,

"And here I thought I was stubborn… this one's in an entirely different league."

Then he drifted off to sleep.

At 7 a.m., his phone rang again. Groggily, he answered.

"Hello?"

Arifa's anxious voice came through:

"Assalam-o-Alaikum, beta. I'm so sorry to call so early, but my friend went to the airport—waited for two hours—Khadija never showed up. Wasn't her flight from Ankara supposed to land at 5 a.m.?"

Now fully awake, Zafir sat up.

"Wa Alaikum Assalam, Aunty. I'm sorry—I didn't get the chance to inform you. Actually, just last night, Khadija called. She said a friend had arranged a place for her, and she'd be staying with them instead."

Arifa exhaled in relief.

"Alhamdulillah! So she has a decent roof over her head.

Do you have the number of that friend?"

"No, I'm afraid I don't," Zafir answered honestly.

"Alright, beta. If you hear from Khadija again or get a contact number, please let me know."

"Of course, Aunty."

Then, with slight hesitation, Arifa said,

"Beta, can I ask something... and will you agree?"

"Yes, Aunty. Please go ahead."

"Whatever happens, please don't mention Khadija or anything about her to anyone around you—especially not to your father's friend."

Zafir raised an eyebrow.

"Okay... I won't. To be honest, I don't have much interaction with him anyway. We only talk over the phone occasionally. But it sounds like you know him?"

Arifa responded vaguely,

"Let's just say… something like that.

Alright, beta, I'll end the call now. May Allah keep you safe and protect you from all harm. Allah Hafiz."

Scene 97

A New Gudiya

"How are you, Gudiya? It's been a while since you called," Zafir greeted cheerfully.

Saira's voice beamed through the receiver:

"Bhai jaan! I had good news to share. I told Mummy to tell you, but she said, 'You're closer to your brother than anyone, so you should be the one to share it.'"

Zafir's voice lit up with excitement.

"What is it? Tell me quickly!"

"You're officially Mamoo jaan now—to a beautiful baby girl!" Saira announced joyously.

"Mashallah, congratulations! Where's Kashif? Let me congratulate him too," Zafir said, beaming.

"He's out at the moment," she replied with a smile in her tone.

Zafir chuckled:

"So, now my Gudiya has a little Gudiya of her own. I wish I could fly over right now to meet you all and hold your tiny princess."

They talked for a long while—savouring the happiness, for once untouched by shadows.

Scene 98

A Knock at the Quiet Door

A few weeks later, on his father's advice, Zafir enrolled in a university in Islamabad. His days began to settle into a routine—studies, solitude, and a steady rhythm. In all that time, neither Arifa nor Khadija reached out.

One evening, as Zafir studied in his apartment, the doorbell rang—an unexpected interruption.

He peeked through the door viewer—

To his surprise, it was Babar Durrani and his family.

He quickly opened the door, greeted them warmly, and welcomed them in.

"Seems like you've gotten so busy in Islamabad, you forgot about us," Babar Uncle said with a smile.

Zafir returned the smile,

"No, Uncle—it's not that. I recently enrolled in university here. They accepted my previous credit hours, so I started directly from the sixth semester. It's a pretty intense workload right now. How are all of you?"

Mrs. Durrani looked at him with warm approval,

"Beta, you should visit us sometime too—that's your home as well."

Zafir replied politely,

"Of course, Aunty. As soon as I get a break, I'll drop by. And really, you didn't have to bring pizza and all these treats!"

Babar said affectionately,

"You're living here alone. We figured we'd share a meal together for once."

Over dinner, Mrs. Durrani introduced her daughter:

"This is our daughter Bina. She's just started in Fine Arts—at your university, actually."

Bina soon struck up a conversation with Zafir, and the evening wore on in easy conversation.

Eventually, they left, leaving Zafir alone once more—still unaware of the tangled threads quietly weaving between his life and a past none of them have yet dared to name.

Scene 99

The Invitation Below

Khadija had found a quiet rhythm again—living in the upper floor of Aamna's house, enrolled in an online graduation program, cocooned in silence that she'd chosen for herself. Aside from a brief call with Arifa that brought measured peace, she kept to her space.

But with the wedding season blooming, that stillness broke. Aamna's home filled with chatter, relatives, and festivity. When guests overflowed into the upstairs floor, Khadija didn't object—but neither did she mingle.

Among the guests was Aamna's khala's family from Multan—including Tahir, a final-year med student who had come for his cousin's wedding and was dutifully helping with the preparations.

One afternoon, Khadija stepped out of her room, headed somewhere when she unexpectedly came face to face with Tahir. He smiled, casual but not impolite.

"So you're Aamna's friend—the famously elusive one?"

Khadija replied in a flat tone,

"Correct. I don't get chummy with people."

She started to walk away, but Tahir added,

"There's a difference between avoiding familiarity and being... abrasive. Seems like you don't even tolerate small talk."

That stopped her. She turned slightly, eyes narrowing.

"What's that supposed to mean?"

Tahir's voice softened.

"Khala jaan—uh, Aamna's mom—and everyone downstairs are waiting for you. We're leaving for the mehndi event. I just came up to grab my car keys, and they asked me to call you down.

By the way, I'm not great with people either."

Without waiting for a response, he turned and headed down.

Khadija stood for a moment, absorbing the encounter. Something in his last line—quiet, unforced—eased the stiffness in her posture.

Then, wordlessly, she began descending the stairs.

Scene 100

Equations and Proposals

Within a short time, most of Zafir's professors came to realize he was no ordinary student. Quiet, focused, brilliant—his intelligence left an impression. One afternoon, as he was leaving class, his Power Electronics professor called him into his office.

Zafir entered and sat down as Professor Haroon said,

“We’ve received a research grant from SUPARCO. It’s a project on Aerial Remote Sensing. Professor Nizami is heading the main program, but the power supply design portion has been assigned to me. I’ve observed you in class more than once, and I believe you have real potential for research. Would you be interested in joining this project?”

For Zafir, it was like a prayer answered. He hadn’t expected a research opportunity in his dream field to land in his lap while juggling studies. Elated, he replied,

“Sir, I’m absolutely ready.”

“Good,” Professor Haroon said. “Once the paperwork’s in place, we’ll have a kick-off meeting and begin work.”

Zafir hadn’t shared anything about his past or prior research—but here was opportunity reaching for him on its own. He returned to his apartment and immediately called Saira.

Bursting with excitement, he told her everything.

“Mashallah, Bhai jaan. That’s wonderful,” she replied. “May Allah bless you with success. I’m genuinely so happy for you.”

"I'm thrilled too," Zafir said. "I spoke to Mummy yesterday—Shakir has started his job, Alhamdulillah, and Zakir should be joining soon after his results are out."

"Yes," Saira said. "Mummy told me that as well. And she said something else..."

Zafir perked up.

"What is it, Gudiya?"

Saira chuckled.

"She said Daddy spoke to his friend—Uncle Babar Durrani—about something to do with his daughter Bina and... you."

Zafir blinked.

"What... what about me?"

"I'm surprised you don't already know," Saira said. "I thought this was being discussed with your understanding. I assumed you were on board."

Zafir's voice shifted, slightly tense.

"I'm shocked Daddy didn't even talk to me about something this important. And Gudiya—you'd know before anyone if there was any such plan on my end."

Saira paused. Then asked lightly,

"So... how is Bina? You don't like her?"

Zafir said honestly,

"It's not that. She seems like a nice girl... I just never looked at her that way. Lately, Uncle and Aunty have been visiting a bit more, and they've invited me over a few times. I guess... I just didn't realize what was on their minds."

"Hmm," Saira said. "Well, if Daddy is considering it, I'm sure he has your best interest at heart."

Zafir went quiet for a moment. Then, softly:

"Alright Gudiya. Take care of yourself, Kashif, and our little princess, Safiya. We'll talk soon. Allah Hafiz."

Scene 101

Glances from the Rear Seat

During Aamna's wedding, several women discreetly asked her mother about Khadija—was she her daughter? Some were scouting for brides for their sons.

But when Aamna's mother clarified that Khadija was simply her daughter's friend, staying temporarily with them because she had nowhere else to go, most of the interest faded quietly.

After the wedding and Aamna's departure, the family began preparing to leave. Aamna's mother said,

"Khadija, ride with Jameela. I'll go in the other car with Aamna's father."

Jameela, Aamna's sister and Tahir's mother, sat in the front seat with her son driving. Khadija sat in the back with Jameela's younger daughter, Farhana.

Farhana glanced at Khadija and asked,

"You're always so quiet, aren't you?"

Khadija replied gently,

"Yes, I'm naturally a reserved person."

Farhana continued,

"Everyone at the wedding seemed so happy, laughing and mingling. But I didn't see you smile… not even once. And you're Aamna baji's good friend."

Before Khadija could respond, Jameela interjected from the front:

"Farhana, that's not polite. Some people are quiet by nature. Not everyone is as chirpy as you."

Farhana fell silent.

Khadija then said softly,

“I’m sorry—I’m not very comfortable being overly casual or familiar with people. But it’s not because I’m arrogant or rude.”

Jameela quickly reassured her,

“Of course, dear. We should accept people for who they are, not force them into molds shaped by our own preferences. Don’t take Farhana’s words to heart.”

Scene 102

What We Think, What We See

When they reached home, Khadija quietly retreated to her room.

Tahir, however, spoke up—irritated.

"Ammi, Farhana was absolutely right. And you shut her down for no reason."

Jameela answered calmly,

"Sometimes, beta, saying the right thing at the wrong time does more harm than good."

Tahir frowned.

"What do you mean by that?"

She explained:

"First, Farhana hardly knows her. You don't ask personal questions like that without a relationship to back it. And even if she wanted to ask, she should've done it privately—not in front of everyone. Khadija was clearly uncomfortable, so I intervened to close the matter gently."

Still annoyed, Tahir muttered,

"That's fine, but who does she think she is—with that attitude? She can't just pass off her rudeness and volatility by calling herself an introvert."

Jameela glanced at him quietly.

"Why are you so worked up about her?"

Tahir folded his arms.

"I don't care about her."

She held his gaze.

"I haven't lived this long without learning to read people. I know what happened to that girl. Your khala told me everything—the hardships, the betrayal, the pain she's endured. Given all that, her behaviour seems more than understandable. And if I'm honest… I thought she'd be a good match for you."

Tahir's eyes widened,

"What?! She can barely string a sentence together without flaring up! And you were considering her for me? Why?"

Jameela replied in a measured tone,

"Don't worry—I was only thinking it. But she's not interested in marriage at all. In fact, I think she's almost averse to the idea. Likely because of what her childhood shaped her to expect.

Anyway, forget her for now. Tomorrow, go pick up my and Farhana's outfits from the tailor—we need them for the valima."

Tahir fell into silence—mind distracted now, pulled into thoughts he hadn't expected to entertain at all.

Scene 103

Crossroads of Views and Vanilla Swirls

As Zafir stepped out of the university and headed toward the parking lot, he saw Bina approaching.

She came closer and said casually,

"Hello, looks like you're heading back to your apartment?"

"Assalam-o-Alaikum," Zafir replied. "Yes, classes are over for the day, so I was heading home. How are you?"

"Wa Alaikum Assalam. I'm fine. But my driver called and said there's been a small accident, so he'll be late. I spoke to my dad—he said I should check if you could drop me home?"

"Of course," Zafir said. "Is your driver and car alright?"

"Yeah, he said a pickup truck hit the back. The bumper and lights are broken."

As they walked to his car, Zafir commented,

"Honestly, people here have no regard for traffic rules or road safety."

Bina laughed,

"That's how things are here. You'll have to get used to it."

Zafir glanced at her.

"We shouldn't 'get used to' bad habits. We should work to change them."

Bina, still smiling, said,

"Well, you're from Canada. People there probably follow laws and systems. No one here thinks like that.

You're going back after graduation, right?"

They had gotten into the car by then. Zafir replied,

"Haven't decided yet."

Bina spoke with sudden excitement,

"I really like Canada. What do we even have in this country? It's just... useless."

Zafir turned to her, surprised.

"You're saying that? You've lived in Pakistan all your life. Your family is well-settled and privileged here. Why speak like that?"

"What, don't you like Canada?" she asked defensively.

"I never said that," Zafir replied. "I've practically grown up there. That's my home, in many ways. I've barely lived in Pakistan.

But still—how can someone enjoy the security and resources of a place and then call it worthless? Especially someone who's never had to suffer here?"

Bina met his gaze.

"Let's leave these dry topics. Want to grab ice cream somewhere?"

Zafir gave a half-smile.

"Okay. Sure."

Scene 104

Wires and Windows

The internet had stopped working. Khadija approached Tahir for help, but he replied with casual indifference,

"Call the service provider. What can I do?"

Khadija answered softly,

"I asked Aamna's father to call them since the connection's under his name, but he said he's too busy and suggested I ask you."

"Fine, I'll get the number from him and call," Tahir said.

"I have the number," Khadija added, "but their tech terms confuse me. Last time I called, they told me to reset the rotor and change the password… I have no idea how to do all that."

Tahir smirked.

"It's called a router, not rotor."

"Yes, that." She handed him the number.

"Can you call and fix it today?"

"I'll call them tomorrow," he said.

Khadija hesitated,

"I need to take a class with my students today. I already had to cancel the last one because of the internet."

Surprised, Tahir asked,

"Students? What students?"

Khadija, now visibly frustrated, replied,

"Some children I teach online. Can you please help me get it fixed today?"

"Okay, I'll call now."

An hour later, the internet was working again.

Tahir asked,

"It's working now, right?"

"Yes. Thank you."

Then, after a beat, he said,

"I helped you out—can I ask one question?"

"Go ahead," she said flatly.

"My khala just told me you teach online for five hours a day. Why?" He curiously asked.

Khadija replied quietly,

"Uncle and Aunty let me live in this big house without charging rent. They could be earning thousands every month. I can't accept all this for nothing, so I contribute whatever little I can. And..."

She paused.

"And what?" Tahir prompted.

She drew a deep breath.

"And... someone once helped me. I owe him. I'm saving money to pay him back."

A trace of guilt softened Tahir's face.

"Oh... I'm sorry. I misjudged you."

Scene 105

A Shadow Beneath the Applause

After four months of intensive work, the research project concluded with exceptional results. SUPARCO officially commended the team, noting especially the innovative contributions from Zafir. Professor Haroon and others were deeply impressed by his intellect and quiet resolve.

Then, a few days later, Professor Haroon received an unexpected call from SUPARCO's Research Director.

After formal greetings, the Director said curtly,

"There's something important we need to discuss."

"Of course," Haroon replied. "Will you visit me or should I come to your office?"

The Director's tone turned cryptic:

"The meeting is scheduled for tomorrow—1 p.m.—at the FIA office."

Haroon froze.

"FIA?" the word escaped him almost involuntarily.

The Director continued calmly,

"You understand the sensitive nature of our work. All individuals associated with these projects are subject to detailed background checks. Since your team involved students from multiple departments, the process took time.

We didn't halt the project, but checks were ongoing in parallel. And you might be surprised to know—all came through clean... except one."

Haroon's voice held concern.

"Who?"

"Zafir Suhban," came the quiet reply.

Haroon was stunned.

"Zafir? But he's one of the sharpest minds I've seen. If it wasn't for his idea and dedication, the power supply module wouldn't even exist. There was a point when everyone was ready to abandon the design—and it was his effort alone that revived it."

The Director's voice softened but stayed firm:

"I don't doubt his brilliance. But FIA flagged him. That means there's something—something you or I might not be aware of.

Which is why Special Investigation Officer Jawad Mehboob has called both of us to the FIA headquarters tomorrow."

Scene 106

The Whisper Beneath the Wind

"Beta, we've planned a grand dinner at a restaurant in Daman-e-Koh this weekend for family and friends. You must come," Babar Durrani had said over the phone.

Zafir had wanted to decline, but Uncle Babar's warm insistence left him little room.

The gathering was at a beautifully appointed restaurant nestled in the hills of Margalla. The air was crisp, the city lights below scattered like spilled stardust.

Babar Durrani introduced Zafir to the relatives one by one:

"This is the son of my childhood friend, Farooq Suhban. He's come from Canada to study here."

Then turning to Zafir, he said,

"Beta, this is my middle brother Javed, and this is the youngest, Liaqat. That's our only sister Kulsoom and her husband Jabbar."

Zafir greeted each of them with a warm handshake and smile.

"So you're three brothers and a sister. Funny—our family's the same: three brothers and one sister."

Liaqat added,

"We were actually four. Our elder brother, Ramzan, lived in Sharjah. He passed away, so now it's just us three."

"Sharjah... Ramzan..." The names struck something in Zafir. He couldn't immediately place it, but they echoed somewhere in his mind.

Javed then asked,

"So, beta—most people leave Pakistan to study in America or Canada, and you did the opposite?"

Zafir smiled politely.

"Some circumstances came up, and Daddy and I thought it best for me to do my undergrad here. I'll pursue my master's or PhD in Canada or the US."

He was still engaged in conversation when he overheard Babar Durrani talking to someone nearby:

"Yes, this is the boy we've chosen for Bina. In-sha-Allah, we'll soon announce their engagement in a grand ceremony."

Zafir froze momentarily. Though it was said in passing, it struck deeper than he expected. After dinner, he quietly stepped away to a quieter, open-air spot—looking out over the glittering sprawl of Islamabad.

That's when a voice broke his solitude.

"Why are you standing here all alone?"

Startled, Zafir turned. It was Bina, smiling gently.

"Just wanted some fresh air," he replied.

"Honestly, I've never attended such a lavish gathering in my life. Back at my sister Saira's wedding, we only had two dishes. It was nothing like this."

Bina laughed softly.

"We're used to these kinds of events… but if you don't enjoy them, then I don't either."

Zafir blinked.

"What do you mean by that?"

Still smiling, she waved it off.

"Let's skip the heavy talk. Come on, let's head up—there are some local jewellery stalls. Let's check them out."

"Okay," Zafir said with a half-smile—and followed her into the softly lit night, the city glittering quietly at their backs.

Scene 107

The Gift, the Proposal, and the Punchline

"This is for you," Tahir said, handing over a small box.

Khadija looked puzzled.

"What is it?"

"A wireless internet device. In case the main connection breaks down again, you won't have any trouble with your classes."

Khadija replied calmly,

"Thanks. But I don't want it."

Tahir blinked.

"Why? It's useful for your work."

"It is—but I'll buy it myself. I can't take it from you."

"Then take it as a gift," he offered.

Her voice remained firm.

"I don't accept gifts from strangers. Sorry."

She turned to leave.

From behind, Tahir raised his voice slightly,

"Alright then—accept it as a sign of friendship?"

Still walking, Khadija said without turning,

"I don't believe in friendship with boys. I've only made one friend in my life—and that's your cousin Aamna."

Just before vanishing down the hallway, she paused.

"One moment, please," Tahir called after her.

She turned.

"Yes?"

Tahir spoke rapidly,

"My final year in medical school has begun. I'll be a doctor in a year. Then a house job... maybe a posting abroad."

Khadija snapped,

"And why are you telling me all this?"

He didn't flinch.

"Because I want to marry you."

"WHAT?!" she exclaimed, stunned.

"Yes. I know my khala might've hinted at it before, but you never gave a clear answer, so..."

"So you thought you'd buy me off with favours and sneak your proposal in?" she interrupted angrily.

Tahir flustered,

"No—it's not like that. You're an adult, independent... I didn't think talking to you directly would be inappropriate."

"It is—because I hate the words 'marriage' and 'husband'," she spat, and stormed off.

After a beat, a voice chirped nearby:

"Wow, Tahir bhai, that was... intense."

Tahir turned to see his younger sister Farhana, grinning.

"You were eavesdropping?" he grumbled.

"Not eavesdropping," she teased. "I was enjoying a live screening of 'The Great Rejection: Dot Com Edition.'"

"You're going to get it from me!" He sharply said.

She laughed,

"Careful! If you lay a finger on me, I might slip and tell Amma how the 'arrogant madam' shut down your proposal like a courtroom verdict."

"Fine—keep it quiet. Don't tell anyone. Not even Mom."

"Sure," she said sweetly. "But it'll cost you. Twenty-five thousand—or a designer outfit of my choice."

"Greedy girl," he muttered. "Fine, just zip it. Or everything will fall apart."

Farhana giggled,

"Wait… you still think this can work out?"

Tahir smiled faintly,

"From how decisively she said 'no,' I have a feeling… she might say 'yes' someday with the same force."

Scene 108

Flagged by Silence

"Please, have a seat," said FIA Officer Jawad Mehboob as Professor Haroon and SUPARCO's Research Director entered the office.

Once seated, Officer Jawad asked bluntly,

"How long have you known Zafir Suhban?"

The Research Director, visibly uneasy, said quickly,

"I've only known him for three months. I mentioned that earlier."

Professor Haroon replied with calm confidence,

"And I've known him for about a year."

The officer met Haroon's gaze.

"And what exactly do you know about him?"

"That he's a remarkably bright, hardworking student. He joined directly in the sixth semester of our program," Haroon said.

Jawad's tone shifted—mocking.

"That's all? And yet you gave him access to highly sensitive research?

No personal stake involved, Professor?"

Haroon bristled.

"What kind of baseless accusation is this?"

He turned to the Director,

"Please tell them—Zafir played a crucial role. Without his idea and effort, the power supply model wouldn't have been completed."

Before the Director could speak, Officer Jawad interjected,

"Vouching for him doesn't clear him.

We suspect he's affiliated with a foreign agency or intelligence network. No prior records were found in Pakistan.

Upon deeper checks, we discovered that 22 years ago, a manual passport was issued for him in Rawalpindi. He was a child then—but it was never renewed. He never obtained a Pakistani ID card either.

Recently, however, he was issued a NICOP—by the Pakistani Embassy in Vancouver , Canada.

Further checks reveal he holds dual citizenship, yet nowhere—not even in university forms—has he disclosed that he is also a Canadian national. Why the secrecy?"

There was a long pause before Haroon replied, swallowing hard:

"I... I didn't know any of this. He always struck me as a quiet, exceptional student."

Jawad's tone turned cutting.

"Spies are often brilliant. That's the point."

"W-what happens now?" Haroon asked hesitantly.

Jawad's voice was cold and precise.

"Your record is clear. You've nothing to worry about.

But the boy is suspicious. Until we have definitive evidence, he will remain under observation. And we'll need your cooperation to monitor his activities.

And one more thing—what's been said in this room must stay here."

Scene 109

The Gathering Storm

"Brother, you're out here celebrating your daughter's wedding while a disaster waits to erupt back there," Javed said with a voice weighted by dread.

Babar Durrani, his older brother, turned sharply.

"What happened? Why are you so agitated?"

"Liaqat saw Khadija yesterday—walking out of a bank," Javed said, worried.

Babar scoffed, "What nonsense is this? That girl was supposed to be stranded in Turkey. Why on earth would she be here?"

"Brother, you live in delusion. Liaqat told me himself. He followed her after she exited the bank."

Now it was Babar's turn to grow serious.

"This is dangerous. If she contacts the police or files a case, we're finished. What should we do?"

Javed's voice grew tense.

"I told you back then—why did you have to spin such an elaborate scheme just to claim our late brother's inheritance? You insisted it was the safest route. And now—humiliation and prison are staring us in the face."

Before he could finish, Babar cut him off.

"Fine, enough. There's no point being so defeatist. The plan you and Liaqat suggested back then—the one I rejected—we'll go through with it now."

Javed grumbled,

"Back then, it could've been handled quietly—without suspicion.

Now... it's already gone too far.

Anyway, I'll talk to Liaqat. He knows someone."

Scene 110

The Exit Ramp

One afternoon, Zafir left the university early—some of his classes had been cancelled. As he reached his car and started the engine, he noticed someone tapping on the trunk. He turned—

It was Bina, smiling.

"Hey! Headed back to your apartment?"

Zafir blinked.

"Uh… yeah. You're here? Your classes are over already?"

Bina grinned.

"Nope. I bunked the rest."

Zafir's eyebrows arched.

"You bunked class? Why? That'll set you back academically."

Bina dismissed it with a laugh,

"Oh, I don't stress about studies. Forget all that—what do you say, movie time? I heard there's a great English flick playing."

Zafir looked baffled.

"You skipped class… to go see a film? Well, if that's your choice, I won't stop you. But I'm headed home to study."

"Ugh, study, study. What's the point if there's no fun in life? Come on, let's go together!" she insisted playfully.

Zafir smiled faintly but shook his head.

"You find your joy in entertainment. Mine's in science and research. So I'll be going. See you around. Allah Hafiz."

And with that, he eased the car into gear and drove off—leaving behind more than just a missed movie.

Scene 111

Her Voice in the Dark

Though Khadija rarely left home, she did occasionally go to the bank to withdraw money transferred by the parents of the children she taught online. One afternoon, after withdrawing cash from an ATM, a car screeched to a halt beside her. Two armed men stepped out and pointed a gun at her.

Startled, Khadija handed over her purse silently.

But one of them sneered,

"We don't want the money. We want you. Get in the car. Try anything smart, and you're dead right here."

Trembling, she hesitated.

They shoved her into the backseat, pinning her between them. One barked to the driver,

"Go. Now."

Frightened, Khadija pleaded,

"I only have that money—please, take it and let me go."

One of them replied coldly,

"We're not letting you go. We've been paid to keep you."

As the car turned off toward the tangled alleys of Rawalpindi, one man's phone rang.

A voice on the other end said,

"Keep her death quiet. She should vanish and make it clean."

"Don't worry," the thug answered. "We're taking her to our hideout inside Rawalpindi. It'll be done."

Khadija sobbed,

"Please... I have nothing... no valuables..."

But the man snapped,

"The people who hired us have sentenced you. Our payment is you. So shut up."

As they entered a narrow alley, a motorbike suddenly crashed headlong into their car. The rider flew onto the hood. One thug stepped out, cursing—and that was Khadija's moment.

She bolted.

Though one of them lunged to grab her, she slipped away and dashed through the maze of streets.

She eventually reached a construction site, scaled a barricade blindly—and fell.

When she regained consciousness, she found herself in a dark basement. Weak light streamed through a small window. Her body was scraped and bleeding; one foot felt shattered with pain. She had landed in an unfinished home, in a skeletal concrete space where the wooden scaffolding had collapsed behind her.

The men searched, but eventually gave up and left.

Khadija tried to stand, but the pain was unbearable. Her fear was eclipsed only by the realization: she didn't know if she could get out.

She checked her bag—her phone was there, battery low.

With trembling hands, she called the only person she could:

"Ammi... please... save me. I'm trapped in a dark room."

Arifa's heart stopped.

"My child! Where are you? What happened?"

"Some men kidnapped me. I escaped... fell into some basement... I can't get out... I can't breathe, Ammi, please..."

Arifa's hands went cold.

"I'll get you out, baby. Just tell me where you are."

"I don't know… maybe inside some building under construction in inner Rawalpindi."

Arifa begged her to look for a sign.

With immense effort, Khadija climbed a stool and peered out the high window.

A name. She spotted a restaurant sign—Khuzdar.

"Ammi… the place across from me… it says Khuzdar on the board…"

The line went dead.

Arifa gasped. Khadija's battery had died.

She redialled. Nothing. The number was off.

Panic surged through her.

She called her brother—but he dismissed her coldly:

"I'm not wandering through Rawalpindi just because she wouldn't stay with us. Give me an address, I'll go. Otherwise don't call again."

And hung up.

She called her friend Zarina. No answer—Zarina was away with family in Faisalabad.

Alone, Arifa dropped the phone. Her chest heaving, she wailed,

"Ya Allah, protect my daughter…"

And then—

A spark of thought leapt through her like lightning.

Scene 112

The Window of Mercy

Zafir had returned after offering the Isha prayer, eaten dinner, and was immersed in his university studies.

Sleep crept over him, and just as he lay down, his phone rang.

He saw the call was from Sharjah. He immediately knew—it must be Khadija's mother.

Picking up, he began,

"Assalam-o-alaikum, Aunty... it's been a while since you called—"

Before he could finish, Arifa, choking in tears, said,

"Save my daughter... Please, beta, for God's sake, save my daughter..."

Then she broke down completely.

Zafir sat up, startled, heart racing.

"Aunty, what happened? I promise I'll do whatever I can, In-sha-Allah. But please—tell me what's wrong."

Through her sobs, Arifa managed,

"I've been a terrible mother... and now my daughter is suffering because of me..."

Zafir reassured her,

"Don't say that. Just tell me what happened—Allah will help."

After explaining everything, Arifa pleaded,

"Beta, you're my last hope... may Allah reward you for this kindness, in this life and the next."

Without wasting another second, Zafir said,

"I'm on my way now, Aunty. Don't worry—I'll call you in an hour or so."

He jumped into his car, drove to Rawalpindi, and then froze—he knew how to get to the city, but not how to navigate its maze-like inner neighbourhoods. He didn't have an exact address, only a faint clue.

He stepped out, hailed a taxi, and said,

"I need to go to inner Rawalpindi."

The driver nodded.

"Fine, but where exactly?"

"Just drive. I'll explain." He said.

The inner city's narrow lanes spun around him like a labyrinth.

"Ya Allah... is this a city or a maze? Where will I find her?" he muttered.

The driver overheard.

"Did you say something, sir?"

"No... just stop here." He said.

The meter read 1,500 rupees.

Zafir pulled out a crisp 15,000 note bundle.

"Take this. I need to find a place urgently. I don't know the exact address. All I know is—it's near a construction site across from some restaurant with the word Khuzdar in the name."

The taxi driver frowned,

"Is that place in inner Rawalpindi?"

"Yes."

The driver nodded.

"Alright, we'll search the whole area. Don't worry—I know these streets like the back of my hand."

Arifa called twice during the ride. Zafir kept his voice calm.

"Aunty, I'm still searching. Just keep praying. We'll find her, In-sha-Allah."

After nearly two hours of combing alleys, the driver suddenly stopped.

"Sir... that's Khuzdar Hotel. And across from it—there's a construction site. Might be an unfinished home."

Zafir jumped out.

"This is it. Yes, this is the place."

"Shall I wait?" the driver asked.

"Please do. I'll pay extra." He promptly said.

It was 1 a.m. The neighbourhood was deserted. Zafir circled the site, found the basement opening, and peered into the darkness.

"Khadija...?" he called down.

No answer.

He called again—once... twice... then noticed a faint movement, the softest groan of pain.

Heart racing, he spotted a ladder nearby, dragged it over, and climbed down.

There she was. Crumpled. Wounded. Barely conscious.

He rushed over, gently lifting her to a sitting position. Her eyes blinked open and stared at him, stunned.

“Zafir… you’re… here?” she whispered.

And then she fainted in his arms.

Panic jolted through him. He checked for breath—she was alive.

He carried her on his back, climbed out, breath ragged, and stumbled to the road. The taxi driver rushed to help.

“Who is she, sir? What happened?”

“I’ll explain on the way. Just go—my car’s a little ahead. We need to get her to a hospital.” Zafir uttered.

They sped off. As they drove, Zafir said,

“She had an accident and fell into that basement. Lost consciousness.”

They reached his car. Zafir laid her carefully in the backseat, offered more money, but the driver refused,

“You’ve paid more than enough. It’s fine.”

Zafir thanked him and zoomed off toward Islamabad.

As he drove, he called Arifa.

“Assalam-o-alaikum, Aunty. Alhamdulillah—I found her.”

Arifa wept with joy,

“May Allah bless you always. How is she? Where is she? Please, let me speak to her!”

“She’s here, in the backseat. Still unconscious. I’m taking her to the hospital now. I’ll call you again soon.”Arifa’s prayers followed him into the night.

Scene 113

The Name We Don't Speak

At the hospital, Khadija was treated in the emergency unit. Her wounds were bandaged, and X-rays revealed a fortunate escape—no broken bones. She was then moved to a ward and given a drip.

When Zafir entered, a nurse was checking her vitals.

"How is she now? And why hasn't she regained consciousness?" he asked.

The nurse responded gently,

"She's stable. The medication is keeping her drowsy. Let her rest here overnight, and you can decide in the morning whether to discharge her. Walking will be painful for a few days; her ankle's badly twisted."

Zafir nodded.

"Thank you. It's better she stays here tonight. If she improves by morning, I'll take her home. Otherwise, we'll continue treatment here."

The nurse looked thoughtful.

"How did she fall? The injuries are quite extensive."

Zafir hesitated. Telling the full story didn't feel right.

"She slipped on some stairs," he said, keeping it vague.

The nurse smiled knowingly.

"Don't worry—she'll recover soon. I'll leave you two for now."

As she turned to go, she added with a soft smile,

"You make a lovely couple. May Allah protect you both. Your wife is beautiful—and you're a kind man. Be sure to give charity, just in case."

Before Zafir could correct her—She's not my wife—the nurse was already gone.

He muttered under his breath,

"Pakistanis really love matchmaking..."

Then he called Arifa again and updated her on everything.

"Aunty, she's at the hospital for the night. I'll stay here as well. If she's okay by morning, I'll drop her off at her friend's place and return to my apartment. Please don't worry."

Arifa thanked him profusely, her voice breaking with relief and gratitude, as she showered him with heartfelt prayers from across the sea.

Scene 114

The First Light

Zafir dozed off in the chair beside her hospital bed. Khadija continued to sleep, unmoving through the night.

At Fajr prayer time, Zafir stirred, rubbing his eyes. He looked over—she was still unconscious.

He stepped out of the ward and walked to the small hospital mosque to offer his prayer.

While he was gone, a new nurse came on shift and entered to check the patient. That's when Khadija slowly opened her eyes.

"W-where... how did I get here?" she asked, her voice fragile.

The nurse answered gently,

"My shift just started, so I don't know much. I only know that someone brought you in last night. He's been waiting by your side ever since. He just stepped out a short while ago."

Not long after, Zafir returned.

Seeing her conscious, he exclaimed with relief,

"Thank God—you're finally awake. Are you alright?"

Her voice was faint but steadier,

"Yes, better now. Thank you so much... but how did you find me? And... have you really been waiting here all night?"

Zafir quickly said,

"Let's skip all that for now. I think the first thing I should do is call your mother and tell her you're awake. Then you can speak with her yourself."

Tears welled in Khadija's eyes.

"My mother called you?"

Zafir nodded as he dialled,

"Yes."

When Arifa answered, he said warmly,

"Assalam-o-alaikum, Aunty—Khadija's awake. Here, speak with her."

He handed the phone to Khadija, who, upon hearing her mother's voice, broke down in sobs. Quietly, Zafir stepped out of the room, leaving her with the conversation that now needed no witnesses.

Scene 115

The Vanishing

“You’re all worthless donkeys and mules!” the gang leader roared at his men. “Useless, every one of you—good only for stuffing your bellies! You let a weak girl escape? She fooled you and vanished? Get out of my sight!”

The henchmen scattered, and the man, now simmering, pulled out his phone and dialled.

“Mr. Liaqat… the job couldn’t be completed,” he said coldly.

Liaqat’s voice trembled.

“What do you mean? I gave you all the necessary information!”

The man snapped,

“Yes, and using that information we did pick her up. But she’s clever—slippery as a shadow. She outsmarted my men and escaped. I have no idea where she is now.”

Liaqat’s voice tightened,

“Oh no… what happens now?”

The man replied flatly,

“I don’t know where she fled. If you like, I can return fifty percent of the advance. I failed to deliver what was promised.”

Liaqat hung up, overwhelmed. Silent for a moment, he then called Babar and Javed to share the news.

Scene 116

Manners Between the Lines

Zafir returned to the hospital room a short while later. Khadija had already spoken to her mother and was feeling a little better.

As she handed his phone back, she said softly,

"Thank you so much."

Zafir replied,

"No need. How are you feeling now? If you're well enough, I can drop you home—or if not, just rest here a bit longer."

Khadija said weakly,

"I don't think I have the strength to get up just yet."

Zafir quickly assured her,

"No rush at all. You rest here. I've got to go to university for a bit—once I'm done, I'll come back and, In-sha-Allah, if you're better, I'll get you discharged and drop you off."

Khadija whispered,

"Thank you."

"Okay then," Zafir said. "Rest well. I'll head out. Assalam-o-alaikum."

A beat later, Khadija responded faintly,

"Okay."

He paused at the door, turned with a slight smile and said,

"Okay' isn't the proper response to Assalam-o-alaikum. It's Wa alaikum assalam. Assalam-o-alaikum."

Khadija lowered her gaze and replied softly,

"Wa alaikum assalam."

Scene 117

The Bridge Called Saira

"I did bring it up with him," Zafir's mother said gently, "but it didn't seem like he was too interested in the proposal."

His father leaned forward,

"I still think this is a perfect match. Babar's been my friend since childhood. They're well-settled, and it would be easier for Zafir to build a life there. Coming back here permanently might actually complicate things for him. Babar's daughter is a good girl—and their family is very eager about this."

His wife nodded thoughtfully.

"That's true. Mrs. Durrani even sent a photo of her. She seems lovely. But I just don't sense that Zafir feels anything for her."

Zafir's father smiled slightly.

"Then bring Saira into this."

"Saira? Why her?" she asked, surprised.

"You're really asking?" he chuckled.

"She may be three years younger, but she's his advisor. He shares everything with her. Take Saira into confidence—ask her to talk to him, feel things out. If anyone can make him see reason… it's her."

Scene 118

Flowers and Forks in the Road

After finishing up at university, Zafir headed straight toward the hospital. On the way, he passed a flower shop. He paused for a moment, thinking, then pulled over. He bought a bouquet and placed it gently in the seat beside him.

Just as he started the car, his phone rang. The number was unfamiliar.

He picked up—and it was Bina.

“Come have evening tea with us today,” she said casually.

Zafir responded politely but firmly,

“Today won’t be possible.”

She pressed on,

“Fine, if you can’t come to us, I’ll come to you! Then we can go out for tea or coffee somewhere nice.”

Zafir glanced briefly at the bouquet.

“That won’t work either. I’m on my way to the hospital—to visit someone who’s unwell.”

Bina said with a light, knowing tone,

“And here we thought we were the only people you knew in town. Clearly, you’ve got other acquaintances too.”

Zafir replied simply,

“Yes, that’s right.

Anyway, I should get going. We'll talk later. Assalam-o-alaikum."

Bina replied with a little smile in her voice,

"Very well then. Wa alaikum assalam."

Scene 119

The Quiet Return

When Zafir arrived at the hospital, he stepped into Khadija's room and found her fast asleep. Without a sound, he placed the bouquet gently near her pillow and stepped back out into the hallway.

He approached the duty nurse to ask about her condition. The nurse glanced at her chart and said,

"She's doing better overall—but she's very weak. Hasn't been eating much, has she? We tried several times, but she barely touched anything. We had to put her on a drip to prevent further weakness. My recommendation? Let her rest here tonight and discharge her in the morning."

Zafir nodded thoughtfully.

"Alright, we'll do that."

As he spoke, his phone rang again. It was Arifa—checking in once more, her worry still heavy in her voice.

Zafir updated her gently,

"Aunty, the hospital staff says she hasn't been eating much, so she's very fatigued. They're suggesting we discharge her tomorrow morning."

Arifa's voice trembled but was warm,

"That's fine, beta. Drop her home tomorrow after she's released.

The way you've stepped up for us—despite not being family—my heart truly prays for you. Your mother deserves praise... she raised a remarkable son."

Zafir's voice softened,

"Thank you, Aunty. I actually spoke to my Mummy yesterday. She misses me a lot. It's been over a year and I haven't seen her since I came here."

"Oh! She must miss you terribly," Arifa said, her voice full of motherly empathy.

"Yes, Aunty, she really does," Zafir replied quietly.

Then she asked,

"Beta, could I speak to Khadija for a moment?"

Zafir answered gently,

"She was in deep sleep when I checked earlier. But In-sha-Allah, I'll let you speak with her later."

He hung up, exhaled deeply, and considered heading back to his apartment. Maybe he'd swing by later to check again, just once before bed.

But something tugged at him—a quiet instinct.

He turned.

And his steps began carrying him back… toward Khadija's room once more.

Scene 120

The Conversation Beneath the Quiet

When Khadija awoke, a nurse was checking her blood pressure and temperature. She noticed the bouquet near her pillow and asked,

"Who brought these flowers?"

The nurse smiled,

"The same person who brought you here."

"Zafir Suhban?" Khadija murmured.

The nurse chuckled,

"You call your husband by his full name? That's rare!"

Khadija blinked, confused.

"What are you talking about?"

The nurse, finishing up, smiled mischievously as she left the room,

"Missing him, aren't you? Well, he's here—went to speak with the head nurse just now."

Outside, Zafir—who had overheard the entire exchange—quickly turned away, muttering,

"These nurses should be working for a marriage bureau."

Moments later, he walked into the room and said warmly,

"Assalam-o-alaikum. How are you feeling now?"

Khadija replied softly,

“Wa alaikum assalam. Much better… and thank you for the flowers.”

“Did you like them?” he asked.

“Yes. They’re lovely,” she said.

Zafir nodded and added,

“Your mother called. Would you like to speak with her?”

“Not just yet… maybe in a little while,” Khadija whispered.

Zafir looked at her gently.

“I’ve been meaning to say something for a while now… but haven’t quite had the courage.”

Khadija looked up.

“What is it?”

Taking a slow breath, he said,

“I think… you’re angry with people. And maybe… with God.”

Khadija’s voice grew low and heavy,

“I’ve only known betrayal and humiliation from the people who should’ve protected me.

And now… someone wants me dead. I have nothing but grief and pain.

Is it a sin if I complain to the One who listens?”

Zafir lowered his gaze,

“I once read: The wounds that don’t show often hurt the most.

And you carry many of them, I think.

May I share a piece of advice?”

Khadija nodded faintly.

He pulled out a book and began reading a passage about forgiveness, detachment from people's opinions, gratitude through hardship, and the power of patience. The words weren't just ink on paper—they were balm.

When he looked up, he saw her silently weeping.

Alarmed, he said,

"I didn't mean to upset you... Should I balance it out with my entire life story?"

She nodded—still teary, but willing.

Zafir told her about his upbringing in Iqaluit, his bond with his sister Saira, and how life had shifted since coming to Pakistan. He confessed how isolated he felt, especially with pressure from his parents to marry Bina—how even at the university, professors had started behaving strangely toward him. There was confusion everywhere.

"Sorry for dumping all this on you," he added sheepishly.

"You didn't. Not at all," she replied gently.

"You're the only person here I can really talk to.

Back in Iqaluit, I talked to Gudiya—my sister—about everything.

But now she's married, has a baby, and I try not to bother her too much."

Khadija smiled softly,

"You really love your sister, don't you? You've mentioned her many times."

He nodded.

"We were best friends. No other kids our age in the area—just Saira, Shakir, and Zakir.

And now that I've told you everything... it's your turn."

Khadija exhaled deeply and began sharing her story. The fractured pieces of her life. A father who saw her as a curse. A childhood of fear and pain. An uncle's betrayal in Turkey. Her sorrow had layered itself so deeply that she no longer knew where grief ended and fear began.

"...and just when I thought things were stable, someone out there tried to erase me altogether."

Zafir saw her wiping tears. He leaned forward instinctively.

"Your uncle left you in Turkey... That still shocks me—"

But before he could continue, his phone rang. It was Bina.

"Look, you dodged today by calling yourself busy," she said playfully.

"But tomorrow, we're grabbing coffee after class—Tim Horton's just opened a branch! Say yes, and no backing out!"

Zafir replied calmly,

"Actually, I don't really drink Tim Horton's coffee. We never had a branch in Iqaluit."

"Then even better—we'll try it for the first time together. That's settled. See you tomorrow."

She hung up.

Zafir stared at the phone, lost in thought.

Seeing him distracted, Khadija said quietly,

"Your uncle's daughter's name is Bina, right?

Funny... my cousin's name is Bina too.

Anyway—I think I'll rest now."

Zafir nodded,

"Sure. I'll head out too. I'll stop by tomorrow before university and drop you home."

Khadija watched him as he turned.

Then she said softly,

"Assalam-o-alaikum."

Zafir smiled and turned back.

"Wa alaikum assalam. Our imam back in Iqaluit always said: 'Entering and leaving with salam adds light to the heart.'

Thank you for reminding me."

He left.

And soon, Khadija drifted into sleep.

Scene 121

The Unyielding Thread

"Ammi, please talk to Khala Jaan again—maybe she can help us with this," Tahir urged.

Jameela sighed,

"Beta, your aunt and I have already spoken. She clearly refused. Without Khadija's consent, we can't force anything on her.

I liked the girl too… but there are things—certain concerns—that now make me hesitant about this match."

Tahir, still insistent, said,

"But that was then. It's been a while since we returned from Islamabad. She might have changed her mind. Just talk to her one more time."

Jameela looked at him with quiet deliberation,

"Fine. I'll try. But you listen carefully, with both your heart and your head: I want to see my son practical and professional. Not some love-struck Majnun. Is that clear?"

Tahir swallowed and nodded,

"Yes, Ammi… it will be exactly as you wish.

But please understand—I truly like her.

Promise me you'll try your best to turn that 'no' into a 'yes.'"

Jameela smiled gently and placed a hand on his shoulder,

"In-sha-Allah, I'll do all I can."

Scene 122

The Interruption

In the morning, when Zafir arrived, he found Khadija already sitting on a chair in her room, ready and dressed.

"You look ready," Zafir said after greeting her.

"Let me just check with the nurse and accounts. We'll be off shortly."

A few minutes later, he returned.

"Shall we go?"

Khadija tried to walk, but it was clearly painful.

Zafir offered gently,

"Would you like me to get you a wheelchair or a walking stick?"

Khadija was struggling with each step, the sprain in her foot making balance difficult.

She replied faintly,

"No, I can manage. The thought of a wheelchair or walking stick just... unsettles me."

Still, walking proved difficult, and she nearly stumbled. Zafir quickly stepped forward, caught her arm, and said with concern,

"You're having trouble keeping your balance. Please wait here—I'll get a walking stick. Just use it for a few days. Once your ankle heals, you can toss it aside."

He returned with a cane, and with its help, Khadija walked more steadily.

As they exited the hospital, Zafir said,

“Wait here. I’ll bring the car to the gate so you won’t have to walk to the parking lot.”

On the way home, Khadija murmured,

“My handbag was left back in that basement. It had my phone… and some money.”

Zafir, hands on the wheel, replied,

“Oh—I completely forgot. Don’t worry, I’ll swing by there sometime soon. If I find anything, I’ll bring it straight to you.”

After dropping her off at home, Zafir set off for university.

But then—

A double-cabin pickup truck swerved aggressively in front of his car and braked hard.

Zafir slammed his brakes to avoid a collision.

Scene 123

The Sudden Roadblock

Zafir rolled down his window and shouted,

“What kind of reckless driving is this? Don’t you know how to drive? You just blocked my way with your pickup!”

A man stepped out of the double-cabin truck and looked Zafir in the eye.

“That was intentional. Get out of the car.”

Startled, Zafir asked,

“What do you mean? Who are you?”

The man flashed a badge.

“FIA—Special Investigation Officer Jawad Mehboob. Step out of the car.”

Zafir obeyed, confused.

“Are you police?”

Jawad locked eyes with him.

“Where you come from, we’re called RCMP. Isn’t that right—in Canada?”

Zafir felt the chill in his spine. He swallowed.

“W-what do you want from me?”

Jawad’s voice was icy.

“The truth. Just the truth. The sooner you talk, the less damage you'll suffer. For now, get in the pickup.”

“W-why should I? I haven’t committed any crime.”

Zafir resisted, uncertain.

Jawad's tone turned menacing.

"If you've done nothing wrong, you've got nothing to fear. But if you have—or even intend to—know this: I don't believe in leniency for spies. I'll turn you into carrion for the crows."

Zafir stammered,

"S-spy? I'm just here to study..."

"If you're as innocent as you say, there's no need to be afraid. But experience tells me you're not what you appear to be.

Enough talk. Get in the pickup."

"Officer... please, I'm innocent..."

"Want me to cuff you and drag you?

No more talk. Just get in."

Zafir got into the pickup, heart pounding.

What new storm had come for him now?

Scene 124

A "Motherly" Concern

"Beta, if Faika and Suleman Bhai weren't in town, you could've called me," Jameela said over the phone.

"Just like Faika is Aamna's mom, I'm like a mother to you too. You went through such a terrible accident, and so much pain..."

Jameela had just learned—through Khadija herself—that she'd been in the hospital for two days.

"Thank you," Khadija replied gently. "I'm doing better now."

Jameela continued,

"How did you manage all alone? Faika won't be able to return to Islamabad for another two weeks. Should I come visit you?"

"That won't be necessary, Aunty," Khadija said kindly. "I'm fine now, truly. But thank you so much for asking."

Jameela hesitated for a moment, then said,

"Actually, I'd called to discuss something important with you. But now that I know you're still recovering, I'll let you rest and call again later."

When the call ended, Khadija sat in quiet thought.

Something about the sudden warmth in that conversation... the way "something important" had been deferred...

She couldn't help but wonder—was this call really about checking in? Or was it about Tahir?

Scene 125

Conditioned Liberty

After the interrogation, Officer Jawad dropped Zafir back at his car. His tone was measured, almost gentle now.

"If what you've told me is true, then there's no need for worry.

But for the time being, you're to remain confined to your apartment.

You are not permitted to leave until your statements are verified.

My men will be outside, in plain clothes. So don't even think about trying to escape."

Zafir nodded, anxious.

"Understood, Officer. But everything I told you is true. I barely escaped with my life that night. And now you people are after me for no reason."

Officer Jawad softened slightly.

"I'm not like the other officers—and that's your good fortune.

It's the only reason I'm releasing you under my own guarantee, even though your story is still under review.

Just pray you never cross paths with the rest of this system.

Now go home—and stay home. Don't step outside unless I personally authorize it."

Zafir hesitated,

"But... my final semester exams are coming up in a few weeks."

Jawad thought for a moment.

"Stay home and prepare.

My men will escort you to and from your exams.

But beyond that—you are not to leave the apartment for any reason."

Scene 126

The Visit Unfiltered

Zafir had just reached his apartment when his phone rang—it was Bina, irritated.

She reminded him of their plan to get coffee at Tim Horton's. Trying to defuse her, Zafir said,

"I'm really sorry. My final semester exams are coming up, and I'm swamped with studying. I've mostly been staying in, barely stepping out."

Bina, unfazed, replied with a teasing smile in her voice,

"Oh please—you're smart enough already! No need to get so stressed.

Alright then—if you can't come out, I'll bring coffee and sandwiches to you. And don't even try to object."

Zafir took a deep breath, paused a beat, then said,

"Fine... you can come. Thanks."

Within the hour, she was at his door.

Zafir glanced nervously at the surveillance detail outside.

He worried they might stop her from coming in—but they didn't.

She entered without trouble, unaware that invisible eyes now followed more than just him.

Scene 127

The Calculus of Arrogance

Babar Durrani sat huddled with his two brothers. Javed, clearly uneasy, said,

"What now? She survived. But she hasn't gone to the police or taken any action. Word is—she's just at home."

Liaqat chimed in,

"Should we try again?"

Babar leaned back, weighing his words.

"I think you two are overreacting. She's not a threat.

She wasn't in a position to act against us before, and she still isn't. Even after Turkey, she stayed out of sight, living in anonymity.

And now—even after you had her abducted—she's still silent and hidden away.

You're giving her too much importance. Leave her be."

Javed frowned,

"What exactly are you trying to say?"

Babar's voice dropped into something more calculated.

"What I'm saying is—she was never a danger to us, and she still isn't.

She has no resources, no support. Why provoke her repeatedly and draw attention?

She's buried herself in obscurity—let her stay buried.

There's no need to make noise and invite police scrutiny unnecessarily."

Liaqat nodded in agreement,

"Javed bhai, I think he's right. We're overreacting.

We've already received our share of the money. Not even Arifa or Khadija know the full extent of what Ramzan Bhai owned.

And we've quietly divided all of it."

Scene 128

The Return

The next evening, Zafir suddenly remembered that Khadija had asked him to retrieve her bag. But how could he go out? His apartment was still under surveillance by plainclothes officers.

A thought struck him—he still had Officer Jawad's number.

He dialled.

"I need to go pick something up. It's urgent, won't take long," he said.

After a pause, Officer Jawad replied,

"Fine—but you'll go with my men, and they'll be with you every moment."

"Understood," Zafir agreed.

When they arrived at the old construction site, Zafir turned to the officers,

"We need to go down. Do you have a torch?"

One of them gave him a look, frowned slightly,

"Yeah, in the car. I'll get it."

Zafir and one officer descended into the basement while the other stayed up above.

After a brief search, they found Khadija's handbag and phone, just where she'd dropped them.

"Alhamdulillah, got what we came for. Let's head back."

That night, Zafir returned to his apartment and quietly placed her phone on charge and her bag on the table.

The next day after his exam, he said to the officers,

“I need to drop these off at someone’s place—can we stop there before heading home?”

They nodded.

At her home, he rang the bell. Khadija opened the door, surprised.

“You?!”

Zafir smiled, offered salam, and handed over the bag and phone.

“Oh—thank you. I thought maybe you hadn’t found them... since I never heard back,” she said.

“It’s just that I’m caught in a strange situation right now,” Zafir explained.

“And between that and final semester exams, I couldn’t make it. Yesterday I got the chance, and they were still there—so I came to return them today.”

“Thank you,” she said quietly.

“Alright then—I’ll head out. Assalam-o-alaikum.”

“Wa alaikum assalam,” she replied, closing the gate behind him.

Scene 129

A Visit with Intent

A few months later, Khadija had fully recovered when the doorbell rang one afternoon. To her surprise, it was Aamna's mother—alongside her sister, Jameela.

Khadija let them in,

"Please, come in..."

Jameela smiled warmly,

"Dear, today we're here to speak plainly."

Khadija raised a curious brow.

Aamna's mother quickly added,

"But remember—there's absolutely no pressure."

Hearing this, Khadija had a hunch what this visit was about. She remained quiet.

Jameela continued,

"You don't have any elder here. Your mother is back in Sharjah. But we've spoken to her—she has no objections."

Khadija's eyes widened.

"You spoke to my mother? When—and how? She didn't mention anything to me."

Aamna's mother replied,

"Just earlier today, before we came over. We got her number from your maternal relatives. She'll probably call you after we leave. But yes—she has no objection to this proposal."

Khadija was stunned. Speechless.

Sensing the silence, Jameela chuckled gently,

"Say something, child. You know here, silence is often taken as consent.

And don't worry—I want to bring you home not as a daughter-in-law, but as a daughter."

Khadija's voice was soft but steady,

"I'd like to speak to my mother first."

Aamna's mother nodded graciously,

"Of course, dear. Speak to her at your own comfort.

We'll stop by again tomorrow. Take care of yourself. Khuda Hafiz."

Scene 130

A Conversation Deferred

"How are you, Bhai jaan?" Saira asked over the phone, her voice laced with concern.

"Gudiya, I'm alright. But it feels like I get out of one storm only to find another waiting with open arms," Zafir replied, weary.

"What happened now? I thought everything had settled down."

Saira's voice tightened with anxiety.

Zafir sighed.

"It had. But now the intelligence people here suspect I'm a spy, working for some foreign agency sent to harm Pakistan."

"Oh my God! Bhai, why don't you come back home? Things are better here now," Saira pleaded.

"I'm under house arrest in my apartment. Can't go anywhere—they're monitoring me 24/7.

The only comforting thing is the officer in charge seems honest. He's promised that if he can verify my story, he'll let me go."

Saira said quietly,

"Ya Allah... please end this trial and protect my brother."

Then she paused, rethinking something.

She had intended to speak about the marriage proposal—Bina's name, the rising pressure—but she sensed this wasn't the moment.

Not now, when the air between them was so heavy with uncertainty.

She silently decided to wait.

“Take care, Bhai jaan. We’ll talk soon, In-sha-Allah,” she said gently.

“You too, Gudiya. Khuda Hafiz.”

And the call ended, unspoken truths folded back between distance and dusk.

Scene 131

No Is Not Ungrateful

"Ammi, how could you make such a big decision about me without even asking me?" Khadija said, voice rising with hurt. "You know how I feel about marriage—the very word disgusts me."

Arifa tried to stay calm.

"My child, you can't live this life alone. You need a strong companion—and that's only possible in the form of a loving and respectful husband.

Fame, money, a job—these are illusions. Girls today mistake them as security, defying the path nature intended. But in the end? All that's left is regret."

Khadija shot back,

"I don't chase those things.

I earn only to survive—because the people who were supposed to support me, shelter me, and protect me never did.

Those who promised kindness left me to die."

Arifa's voice gentled.

"Forget the past, my dear. Move forward. Say yes to this proposal."

Khadija spoke with a loaded calm.

"And what's the guarantee he won't turn out like my father?"

Arifa paused, then said softly,

"No one is an angel… but no one is the devil either.

Your father wasn't just harsh or suspicious—he was mentally and emotionally unwell. That's why he did things most people wouldn't.

Every man has his own flaws. Marriage needs managing, patience, and forgiveness. No one is perfect—you love the whole person, not just the good parts.

And love? Allah puts that in the heart after nikkah.

If you're grateful for that blessing, it flourishes. If you let pride and resentment grow—there's no home left to hold you."

But Khadija wasn't ready.

"I'm not taking that risk."

Arifa tried one more time.

"Just think... they've cared for you with more respect than even your own relatives.

Where others turned away, they welcomed you. That alone deserves gratitude."

Khadija snapped,

"Why does everyone who helps me eventually try to marry me off?"

Arifa kept her patience.

"He's educated. He's going to be a doctor. His family wants this with love and respect.

And trust me—this loneliness of yours isn't meant to last a lifetime. Please... say yes."

But Khadija's voice turned quiet.

"I need time to think. Tell them not to pressure me.

I won't answer directly. But you can speak on my behalf.

Please also ask Aamna's mom to stop visiting so often—it's too much, especially when I'm still living in their house."

Arifa sighed.

"Alright, my dear. I'll talk to them. Don't worry."

Scene 132

Classified Brilliance

"What do you mean by that?" the university chancellor asked, astonished.

They were gathered in a high-level meeting. Present in the chancellor's office were the Head of Zafir's department, the Dean, SUPARCO's Chief Research Director, a Military Research Officer, and FIA's Special Investigation Officer Jawad.

Officer Jawad replied firmly,

"What I said, I said with full responsibility. This young man is an asset, not a threat.

But what I'm about to show you will help you understand why."

He placed before them Zafir's research paper—published in a leading international journal and the Austin University Science Journal.

Zafir's department head gasped,

"Oh my God… this journal is the oldest and most prestigious in science and research.

For Zafir's work to be published here—it's extraordinary."

SUPARCO's Chief Research Director added,

"If the hypothesis in this paper can be turned into a practical device, it would become the greatest scientific breakthrough of the century."

The Military Research Officer nodded slowly,

"Whichever nation develops this first would gain such a technological edge… no rival could match it."

The chancellor looked puzzled,

"If that's the case, then why is this boy even here? Any top global university would snatch him up immediately."

Officer Jawad gave a knowing smile.

"That brings me to the second part of my investigation."

There was a quiet murmur:

"Second part?"

Jawad continued,

"He's a Pakistani-origin Canadian from the remote city of Iqaluit.

After what he went through back home, he came here—quietly, unnoticed, even hiding that he holds dual nationality.

He's been trying to live in peace."

The Military Officer nodded grimly,

"A mind like that is born once in generations.

It's this country's good fortune—even if by accident—that he ended up here.

He must be protected."

Jawad replied,

"So far, no one beyond this room knows anything. I've already arranged for his safety.

But if even the slightest whisper reaches the people chasing him… they will stop at nothing to eliminate him."

SUPARCO's Director offered,

"My recommendation is this:

Let's unite, develop this concept under national interest, and begin immediate R&D.

We'll need significant funding—something that will require state backing."

Jawad nodded,

"One thing: his name cannot be used.

Revealing it could endanger his life."

The Military Officer spoke decisively,

"From this moment forward, he is Scientist X.

That's the only name we use."

Jawad concluded,

"I'll speak to my department—we'll arrange airtight security."

Scene 133

The Visit Reversed

Zafir was completely unaware of the high-level discussions taking place in sealed rooms—of the title now attached to him: Scientist X. He remained under house arrest, the final exams behind him, waiting anxiously for results and wondering how long this confinement would last.

One afternoon, he was reading when his phone rang. The number was unfamiliar. He hesitated, uncertain whether to answer—but eventually picked up with a quiet,

"Hello?"

A familiar voice answered playfully,

"When we meet or part, we start with salaam. Assalam-o-alaikum."

Relief crossed Zafir's face.

"Oh—it's you! Wa alaikum assalam. I didn't recognize the number and panicked for a second. How are you?"

Khadija's tone was composed and clear.

"I'm doing well. You might remember that a long time ago, I asked for your number—so that if I ever managed to repay the debt I owe you, I'd contact you myself. That day has come. That's why I'm calling."

Zafir chuckled softly.

"Ah—I see. You were serious about that?"

"Very much so. A debt is a debt—it only leaves once it's paid. Dreams and intentions don't erase it. So, would you be willing to come over to my place? I'd like to return the money to you in person."

But Zafir's voice turned cautious.

"I'm... going through something complicated right now. I'm under house arrest in my own apartment. The FIA has put me in this situation without cause. So, either we postpone and I collect it later—or if you don't mind, and if it's not inappropriate, you could come here and return it."

Khadija paused.

"I've spent months tutoring children and saving every rupee, waiting for the day I could settle this. If you'd kindly share your address, I'll come to you."

Scene 134

The Gift of Assumption

“Mama… I keep trying to build some understanding between us, but he’s always so cold and passive in his responses,” Bina said to her mother, visibly frustrated.

Her mother replied calmly,

“Sweetheart, some people are just reserved. It’ll be fine after marriage. Your father spoke to Farooq Bhai, and in passing, he hinted that they’re planning to come here for Zafir’s wedding.”

“Really? But you told me the plan was for an engagement first…”

Bina’s tone lifted with excitement.

“Yes, we thought so too. But considering they’ll be traveling all this way, it makes more sense to go ahead with the marriage while they’re here,” her mother explained.

“Wow! That’s even better.

But Mama… I really want Zafir and me to live in Canada after the wedding.

I once brought it up with him, but he didn’t seem too interested.”

There was a hint of doubt in her voice now.

Her mother smiled reassuringly,

“Your dad said Zafir’s degree is nearly complete, so he’s returning to Canada soon anyway.

It's only logical that you go with him. Don't worry—everything will work out just fine."

Those words lit up Bina's face. She went back to her room, thinking.

It had been days since she'd spoken to Zafir—no meetings, no updates.

"Why not surprise him?" she thought.

And just like that, she decided to take a gift and visit him unannounced.

Scene 135

Cleared for Connection

"Sir, there's a young woman. We checked her ID—name's Khadija Ramzan," one of the plainclothes agents informed Officer Jawad over the phone.

They had stopped her outside the building under the guise of security staff, never revealing their real identity. These men had been assigned to protect Zafir by the FIA.

A faint smile touched Officer Jawad's face as he spoke calmly,

"Let her through. She's clean—completely clear. And if she ever comes again, do not stop her. In fact, assign one of our men to discreetly keep watch over her.

She should be protected too. Without her even knowing it."

Scene 136

Uninvited Truth

Seeing Khadija at the apartment gate, Zafir greeted,

" Please come in."

She returned the greeting and handed him an envelope.

"Just take this. I should be going."

Zafir tucked it into his pocket, thanked her, and offered,

"Would've been nice if you stayed for some tea."

Khadija hesitated. Sensing it, Zafir quickly added,

"It's okay—only if you're comfortable."

She nodded softly,

"Alright. I'll have tea."

Once inside the lounge, Zafir said,

"Please sit. I'll make tea. Do you take sugar and milk?"

"Yes," she replied.

"Okay, be right back."

While he was in the kitchen, Khadija noticed the scattered books. Zafir returned with a glass of water, handed it to her and said,

"Tea will be ready in just few minutes."

As she drank, her gaze lingered on the books.

"You really love to read."

Zafir smiled, taking the glass,

"And for that crime, I'm now confined to my own apartment."

Soon he returned with tea. They sat facing one another, sipping quietly. Neither could find the words to start a conversation. Then both blurted out at once:

"The tea is good."

They smiled. Zafir broke the pause,

"How's your mother doing?"

"She's fine. And yours?"

"She's well too, Alhamdulillah."

Silence returned, until Khadija asked,

"How's your little sister?"

Zafir brightened.

"Gudiya is doing great. These days she's always with her little one. Would you like to see a picture of her daughter, Safia?"

"Yes, please."

Seeing the photo, Khadija smiled,

"She's adorable—like a doll."

"Masha'Allah... I miss her so much. Wish I could scoop her up and carry her on my shoulders all day."

"You like children," Khadija observed.

"I do. And Gudiya's daughter is as dear to me as Gudiya herself. Do you like children?"

She nodded.

More silence followed, until Zafir asked,

"Would you like another cup of tea?"

"Sure," she said gently.

He brought more. They sipped again in silence until it was done.

"Thank you," Khadija said. "The tea was nice."

"You're welcome. So… what kind of food do you like?"

"I eat everything. Back when I lived with my grandma, I'd sometimes make requests. Now I cook for myself—just whatever I can manage."

Zafir perked up,

"I love Italian food. My Mummy makes amazing dishes. My favorite's risotto."

Khadija grew thoughtful, a little sad.

Zafir noticed,

"Would you like to try risotto sometime?"

"Are you going to cook it?" She asked.

He grinned,

"Nope—not my skill. But there's a good Italian restaurant nearby. We could go there."

Before she could respond, the doorbell rang.

"Who could that be now…" Zafir muttered, going to answer.

He opened it—and there stood Bina, holding a gift in one hand and two cups of coffee in the other.

"Surprise! Let's sit and talk over coffee!"

She stepped inside.

Zafir panicked for a moment—how would he explain Khadija?

Before he could speak, both women saw each other and blurted in surprise:

"You?!"

"You know each other?" Zafir asked, stunned.

Bina's voice was sharp,

"What's she doing here?"

Khadija had already pieced it all together—Zafir's father's childhood friend was none other than her uncle.

"She's my uncle's daughter. My cousin," Khadija said quietly.

Bina snapped,

"I'm not your cousin. Don't try to claim ties with me. Who knows where Uncle Javed picked you up from? Weren't you supposed to be studying in Turkey? What are you doing here?"

Zafir now realized—Bina's father was the very man who had abandoned Khadija in Turkey.

Khadija rose,

"I should go."

But before she could leave, Bina snarled,

"Hold on—at least explain what you were doing with my fiancé!"

Khadija looked at Zafir. He scrambled,

"I swear, Khadija—I didn't know about any of this."

She looked at him—but said nothing—and turned to leave.

Zafir followed,

"Please, just listen—"

She paused and said softly,

"You don't owe me any explanations, Zafir. You're an honest man. No one knows that better than I do. I have no complaint against you.

If I have any grievance, it's only with fate—for why this always happens to me."

Tears shimmered in her eyes.

"Goodbye. Go be with your future wife.

Assalam-o-alaikum."

And without waiting for his reply, she walked away.

Behind him, Bina scoffed,

"Finally gone. Zafir, you don't know her—she's manipulative. Who knows what spell she cast over my dad and uncle to send her to Turkey with thousands of dollars? No one else in the family ever got such luxuries."

Zafir murmured,

"Luxuries?"

"Yes! A fancy hostel in Turkey? Who paid for that? And when did she even return to Pakistan? Dad and Uncle Javed never mentioned anything. What was she doing in your apartment? And how do you even know her?"

Zafir whispered,

"Oh God..."

"Well?" she pressed. "How do you know that cunning girl?"

Zafir spoke quietly,

"She owed me money—came to return it. We met in Turkey.

I'm the one who helped her get back to Pakistan...

Because some heartless, shameless man left her there to die."

Bina blinked.

"What are you saying?"

He looked directly at her, tone sharp,

"Bina, please go home. Ask your respected father, Mr. Babar Durrani, for the full story.

He'll explain it well."

"What do you mean by that?"

"Please... I need to be alone."

Bina pouted,

"Fine."

She left.

Zafir returned to the couch, sat down—and buried his head in his hands.

Scene 137

A Meeting on Her Terms

Khadija returned from Zafir's apartment feeling deeply unsettled. She lay on her bed, buried her face into the pillow—and cried.

Just a few minutes had passed when the doorbell rang. She quickly wiped her tears with the edge of her scarf and composed herself.

When she opened the door, it was Aamna's mother standing there.

"What happened? Were you asleep?" she asked gently.

"No, Aunty... please come in," Khadija said, stepping aside.

As Aamna's mother settled in, she spoke softly,

"I spoke to your mother. And believe me, I'm not the kind of woman who would pressure you just because you're staying in my house. Truly, there's no such thing in my heart.

If anything, it's just that I genuinely wish for you to be married into a good home soon.

When Tahir's proposal came, I was happy—because I know my sister Jameela very well, and her son Tahir was raised right under my eyes."

Khadija listened silently as she continued,

"But I want to clarify—my intention in talking to you about Tahir was never to pressure you or imply any favour. There's another reason, which I want to explain now."

Khadija looked up,

"What reason, Aunty?"

Aamna's mother exhaled quietly,

"After Aamna's wedding, your uncle and I decided to move to the UK. We already have immigration there, and now that our daughter is settled, we want to sell this house and relocate.

Our only wish was to see you settled in a good place before we go."

Khadija's expression shifted.

"You're leaving? When?"

"Don't be alarmed, dear. Even if your marriage isn't finalized by then, we'll make sure you're settled in a safe place before we go.

We're planning to wind everything up by the end of next month."

"Okay, Aunty," Khadija said quietly.

The older woman reached out gently,

"Don't let this worry you. We'll find you a proper place before we leave. And don't mistake any of this for pressure about marrying Tahir."

Khadija took a breath and said softly,

"Aunty, would it be possible to meet Tahir? I'd like to talk to him."

Aamna's mother lit up,

"Of course! I'll call him today. He'll be here by tomorrow morning, then you two can meet."

Khadija thought for a moment,

"Not here at the house. I'll send you a location. Please ask him to meet me there—tomorrow at 3 p.m."

Aamna's mother nodded, smiling,

"That's no issue at all. He'll meet you wherever you prefer."

Scene 138

The Truth Between the Lines

"Assalam-o-alaikum, Aunty," Zafir said over the phone.

"Wa alaikum assalam, beta. How are you?" Arifa responded warmly.

"Aunty, I have a complaint to make," Zafir said, his voice edged with quiet frustration.

"Complaint? What kind of complaint, dear?" she asked, surprised.

"You knew, didn't you—that the family friend my father mentioned, Babar Durrani... he's Khadija's uncle," Zafir said, trying to contain his anger.

Arifa let out a heavy sigh.

"Yes, beta. I figured it out. But I didn't tell you, because I was afraid it might sour your heart toward them—especially when it was clear from your words that they treated you kindly and had your best interest at heart."

Zafir remained agitated.

"Aunty, those people nearly destroyed your daughter's life—and you didn't even warn me? I kept deepening my ties with them, blind to who they were. Now my parents even want me to marry their daughter."

Arifa said quietly,

"They did wrong to Khadija, yes. It was their hate for me, and for my daughter. But they have no enmity with you. I didn't want to ruin your relationship with them for the sake of my bitterness."

Zafir replied with regret,

"Khadija found out last night. And so did I—right then and there.

She was deeply shaken. And so was I.

Anyway... what's done is done.

I'll go now, Aunty. Allah Hafiz."

Scene 139

Cornered

Babar Durrani was pale and sweating by the time his daughter finished recounting everything that had happened.

“Don’t worry,” he said hastily, trying to reassure Bina.

“I’ll handle it. I’ll talk to him myself.”

Bina looked at him warily.

“But Dad, why did he say I should ask you about all of this?”

Babar tried to dismiss it.

“Maybe he’s upset about something. I’ll explain, and everything will settle down. Now… go to your room. Let me handle this.”

Once she had left, his wife turned to him, clearly suspicious.

“What’s going on? Did you know Khadija is in Pakistan? And why do you look so shaken?”

“W-why would I know? It’s nothing. Just go make me some coffee,” he replied, his voice strained.

Still watching him with narrowed eyes, she said,

“Okay… I’ll bring it.”

The moment she left, he rushed to call Javed.

“We’re finished. It’s a disaster!” he whispered urgently.

“What happened, Bhai Sahib? Why are you so panicked?” Javed asked.

With a mix of anger and dread, Babar muttered,

"That wretched girl of Arifa—Khadija—she's ruined everything."

"What do you mean?" Javed's voice sharpened with concern.

After Babar recounted the entire incident, Javed sighed heavily.

"This is bad… really bad. Here's what you do—come to my place right now. I'll call Liaqat too. We'll sit down and figure out our next move. We need a new plan, fast."

Scene 140

Truth in the Basement Shadows

“Isn’t this a strange place to meet? You actually want to talk at this tiny roadside tea restaurant?” Tahir asked, glancing around uneasily.

Khadija, calm but deliberate, said,

“I brought you here to show you something—and then to tell you something.”

Tahir smiled awkwardly,

“I’m all eyes and ears.”

“Please, come with me,” Khadija said.

She led him around the back of an unfinished house, toward a basement half-hidden in darkness. From above, there was nothing but shadow.

Tahir frowned, uncomfortable,

“What is this? Why did you bring me here?”

Khadija’s voice dropped gently,

“There’s something you need to know. It’s a long story—so I hope you’ll listen all the way through.”

Pointing toward the dim space, she began,

“I was kidnapped. When I escaped their grasp, I stumbled into this very basement. I spent seven or eight hours here.

Those hours... were the most painful of my life. I was injured, terrified, hiding. I thought they’d find me and drag me back.

I didn't know if I'd survive. I cried harder than I've ever cried before in my life."

Her voice grew softer.

"In that darkness, I broke—physically, mentally, emotionally.

I had never prayed before. All I had ever done was complain to God.

But that night, I called on Him—and He answered immediately.

He sent someone I never imagined would come... someone who saved me."

She paused.

"He was the same person who helped me in Turkey, when I was wandering—alone, broke, vulnerable.

He didn't take advantage. He offered nothing but dignity and kindness.

So much so... that I consider my life in his debt."

Tahir stood silent, shaken.

"Who was it?"

"His name is Zafir," Khadija replied softly.

Tahir asked, almost fearing the answer,

"Do you... like him?"

Khadija's eyes didn't waver.

"More than that."

"You love him?"

"Even more than that," she said with unwavering calm.

Tahir swallowed hard.

"Do you... want to marry him?"

Khadija tilted her head slightly,

“Wouldn’t it be fair to ask first what I truly feel for him?”

He nodded.

“And what is it?”

“I respect him. I love him. And I am… deeply devoted to him.”

Tahir’s face turned pale.

“So that’s why you refused my proposal.”

“No.”

He blinked.

“I don’t understand. If you feel this deeply for him, then why?”

Khadija spoke slowly, with a strange sadness,

“Because I’ve always hated the idea of marriage and of a husband.

That feeling hasn’t gone entirely… though maybe it’s fading, slowly.

Still—I owe you an apology. I refused your proposal, despite your efforts and everyone’s requests.

Not because you lack anything. You are well-educated, respectful, from a good family.

You deserve someone wonderful. But that someone… isn’t me.”

She took a breath.

“I asked to meet you here so I could tell you myself.

So that you would step back—yourself—and spare me from saying no to Aamna’s mother.

She's done so much for me."

Tahir nodded slowly, exhaled.

"Okay. I suppose we should go now. Would you like me to drop you home?"

"No, thank you," Khadija said gently.

"You go ahead. I'll take a cab from here."

Scene 141

Scientist X Activated

"Where are you taking me? I've told you a thousand times—I'm not a spy. I've told you everything. Why won't you believe me?"

Zafir spoke with frustration as Officer Jawad drove.

Jawad replied steadily, eyes on the road,

"You're cleared, dear. Don't worry."

"Th-then why did you confine me to my apartment? And where are we going now?"

Zafir asked, growing restless.

Still focused on the windshield, Officer Jawad answered calmly,

"You weren't confined—you were protected.

And where we're going, what lies ahead for you—you'll know very soon."

An hour later, Zafir was seated in a large conference room in an undisclosed building, surrounded by several people.

After briefing him on everything, Officer Jawad said,

"We want you to work for this country."

"What kind of work would that be?" Zafir asked hesitantly.

SUPARCO's Chief Research Director spoke,

"The same idea you proposed in your research paper."

The Military Research Officer added,

"We'll provide every resource and all the security you need."

The University Chancellor assured,

"And we'll offer all the academic and technical support required."

Zafir looked around and asked,

"But do you really think I can advance this kind of research and actually invent something?"

Jawad met his gaze.

"I'm not a scientist. But tell me—do you think you can do it?"

Zafir glanced at him, then smiled faintly. He removed his watch, opened it, and placed a tiny nano chip on the table.

"Everything I developed in Iqaluit—using their resources—is stored in here."

The Military Officer beamed.

"Very good. You're even more competent than we hoped."

Zafir paused.

"But one thing still worries me. If we succeed… won't they come after me again?"

SUPARCO's director replied,

"If we succeed, they won't chase you—they'll be eager to negotiate with us.

And most importantly, your identity will remain secret.

You'll work under the codename Scientist X. No one will know your real name."

The Military Officer elaborated,

"Publicly, we'll claim this invention was developed by our team using your concept. Anyone else can try… but they won't succeed.

It will give our country a decisive edge—one that deters even our strongest enemies."

Officer Jawad outlined the plan:

"You'll remain under our protection in your apartment.

All your movements will be in secure vehicles, and the security personnel assigned to you will wear plain clothes.

A private company will hire you as a design engineer—

Outwardly, it'll seem like you've taken a basic job after graduation.

But within their office, beyond a modest engineering consultancy... there's a hidden bunker where you'll conduct your research."

Zafir nodded,

"I'm ready."

Scene 142

Unravelling with Grace

"He turned it down? But why? Khadija was the one who asked to meet and speak with him," Aamna's mother said in surprise, speaking to her sister Jameela.

"I'm puzzled too. My son was so cheerful before he left, but ever since he returned, he's seemed... deflated," Jameela replied, clearly concerned.

Aamna's mother thought for a moment and said,

"I have a feeling Khadija must've said something that shattered him.

I just don't understand what she objects to. Doesn't she see the circumstances she's in—and that we're simply trying to help her? But she just won't agree."

Jameela responded softly,

"Faiqa, I'm not upset about the rejection.

What troubles me is seeing my son so downcast and distracted.

He claims it was his own decision, that he turned Khadija down... but I think you're right—it was she who refused him.

Still, part of me feels at peace now."

Faiqa looked at her in surprise,

"At peace? Why?"

Jameela explained,

"I only pursued the proposal because of Tahir's insistence.

But there are so many things about Khadija—so many unanswered questions—that would have stirred endless talk among relatives and friends.

Honestly? I now believe it's for the best that it didn't work out."

Scene 143

A Personal Request

Zafir had started working under the guise of a private job while secretly advancing the high-stakes research project. One afternoon, feeling mentally drained, he leaned back in his chair, lost in thought.

After a moment, he picked up his phone and dialled.

Officer Jawad answered,

"What made you call?"

Zafir replied,

"It's a personal matter."

Jawad chuckled knowingly,

"And I'm guessing it has something to do with a young woman named Khadija Ramzan."

Zafir froze,

"W-what… How did you know that?"

"It's our job to know things," Jawad said with a smile.

"And anyone connected to you—we've profiled every one of them.

But tell me—what's going on?"

Zafir sighed.

"There's something I need to share about her. And then… I need a favour."

Jawad's voice turned thoughtful.

"Let me guess—you want to talk about how her multimillion-rupee inheritance was stolen by her uncles, how they left her to die in Turkey, and how someone tried to have her killed just months ago?"

Zafir snapped,

"If you know all this, why haven't you done anything?"

"Because Zafir," Jawad replied calmly,

"we only handle intelligence. The actual investigation and prosecution must come from the police.

But if they open a case and take it to court, your name will surface—and we've gone to great lengths to keep your identity hidden."

Zafir sounded offended,

"So you're saying you'll just sit back and let them get away with it?"

Jawad's tone stayed even.

"Sometimes, to achieve a greater goal, we have to bear smaller injustices.

I'm not minimizing what happened to her—but if we make a move now, your cover could be blown. And that would be catastrophic."

Zafir leaned forward,

"What exactly are you saying?"

"Just this," Jawad said carefully,

"I promise I'll do everything I can to bring those men to justice.

But for now, you cannot involve the police. Not yet."

Zafir took a moment.

"Can I look into it myself? I won't involve the police—I promise."

Jawad considered it.

"Okay. But be extremely careful."

Zafir, now more energized, said,

"Then I need your help.

I want the full documentation of the property that belonged to Khadija—and was stolen from her."

Jawad answered softly,

"You'll have copies of all the files by tomorrow."

Scene 144

The Clock Moves

Khadija was in her portion, teaching children online, when the doorbell rang. She opened it to find Aamna's mother standing there.

"Aunty. Please come in," Khadija said.

"Dear," she replied. "Actually, I just need to speak to you quickly—it's important."

"Of course, Aunty. Shall we go inside?"

"No, no—I'm in a rush. Just listen here," she said gently.

"Your uncle and I have decided to leave sooner than expected. We're moving by the end of this month.

The car and most of the big furniture have already been sold. And just last night, the house was sold too. The new owners want possession by the 19th."

Khadija was taken aback.

"So soon?"

"Yes—the buyers are in a hurry to move in. We want to vacate by the 19th, and our flight to Manchester is booked for the 23rd," Aamna's mother explained.

Concern crept into Khadija's voice.

"But… where will I go? I won't be able to find a suitable place this quickly."

Aamna's mother quickly reassured her,

"Why are you worrying? Didn't I promise that I'd help you settle before we leave?

I have a good friend who's divided her upper floor into four portions.

She'll give one to you. Don't worry about rent either—she won't charge you a penny."

Khadija, with genuine gratitude, replied,

"Thank you, Aunty."

Scene 145

The Call of Conscience

Looking over the documents, Zafir murmured under his breath,

"She owns property worth 250 to 300 million, and yet lives like this—pushed to the margins.

And these wicked men steal her inheritance, trade in her life—and believe no one will ever hold them accountable.

Greed and hatred truly make a person worse than an animal."

He immediately called his father and explained everything. At first, his father couldn't believe it.

"Daddy, these are official records—obtained from police sources. They can't be denied.

And besides, I've seen some of these things with my own eyes.

And yet... you were trying to marry me into that very family."

His father replied, troubled,

"Oh my God. I can't believe this.

But whatever you do, do not confront Babar about this.

I'll call him myself and politely decline the proposal."

Zafir, dismayed, said,

"Not marrying into that family is logical—but barely scratches the surface of what I've told you.

The real issue is giving this wronged girl back what was stolen from her."

His father, growing stern, said,

"You don't need to play judge and jury.

Whatever Babar has done with his niece—it's none of our concern.

And you're not to say a word to him. Understand?"

Zafir replied quietly,

"But I am involved—whether I wanted to be or not.

So yes, I will speak to Uncle Durrani.

I have to step out now. I'll call back later."

After Zafir hung up, his father grew visibly anxious.

Thinking quickly, he dialled Saira.

After the initial greetings, he filled her in on everything and said sharply,

"You need to talk to your foolish and emotional brother. Tell him not to question Babar about this girl.

I'll personally decline the proposal in a tactful way."

Saira replied,

"Yes, Daddy. I'll speak to Bhai jaan this evening. Don't worry."

Scene 146

The Sibling Pact

"Bhai jaan, please… when Daddy is insisting so firmly, can't you just agree to what he's asking?" Saira said gently over the phone.

Zafir's voice held steady conviction.

"Gudiya, you don't understand what those people have done to that girl.

They swallowed up property worth millions of dollars—and that wasn't even the end of it.

They've tried multiple times to have her killed.

And if no one stops them, they'll try again."

Saira tried reasoning.

"But Bhai… isn't that between her and her family?

You said it yourself—she hasn't reported them or taken legal action.

So why are you getting involved in someone else's battle?"

Zafir responded with measured weight.

"This isn't someone else's battle. I'm involved.

You should be on my side.

If something like this had happened to someone in our family… wouldn't you have stood by me then too?"

Saira's voice softened, all hesitation melting.

"Like always, Bhai jaan… I'm with you.

If Daddy calls again, I'll handle it.

Don't worry."

Scene 147

No Questions Asked

"Wa alaikum assalam... It's you! What a surprise—why are you calling?"

Khadija answered, caught off guard but curious.

Without any preamble, Zafir asked,

"Do you trust me , Khadija?"

Khadija responded gently,

"Yes."

"Then if I asked you to come with me somewhere—without asking where or why—would you come?"

His tone was strange. Serious, yet hopeful.

Khadija didn't hesitate.

"Yes. I'd go."

Zafir's voice lit up with joy.

"Then get ready. I'll be at your place in an hour. Just come with me."

Scene 148

Reckoning and Refusal

Khadija greeted with a quiet salam and got into the car. Zafir started driving. Neither of them spoke a word.

When the car stopped outside Babar Durrani's bungalow, Khadija was surprised—why had he brought her here? She'd been to this house before during social gatherings while living with Uncle Javed. Still, she remained silent.

The guard recognized Zafir and opened the gate. He parked and walked around to open Khadija's door.

"Please come with me," he said calmly.

She followed, still uncertain, remembering his request for silence.

Inside the lounge, Babar Durrani and his family were sipping tea and watching TV. Khadija trailed a few steps behind Zafir and wasn't immediately noticed.

"Zafir, dear! It's been so long," Babar greeted warmly.

"Come in, beta, don't stand at the door," his wife added.

Bina, seated nearby, grinned.

"If you've come for me, I'm ready! I skipped tea—we can grab coffee instead."

Zafir motioned behind him.

"Please... come in."

When Khadija entered, Bina shrieked,

"Why did you bring that cunning witch into our house?"

But Babar turned pale at the sight of Khadija beside Zafir. Swallowing hard, he said nervously,

"Let's all talk calmly. You two, come with me."

He tried to lead them away, but Zafir stood firm.

"No, Uncle. Whatever's going to be said—it'll be said here. In front of everyone."

"Why are you trying to escalate this?" Babar pleaded.

Zafir ignored him.

"Uncle Javed and Uncle Liaqat are on their way. It's better if everyone hears this together."

"Y-you called them too?!"

"Yes. With their families. They'll be here any minute."

Khadija watched in stunned silence.

"Zafir, you're crossing a line. I'll be speaking to your father," Babar warned.

"And you and your brothers crossed every line long ago," Zafir shot back.

"What's going on? Someone tell me!" Bina demanded.

Her mother, sensing the storm, hushed her.

"Let your father speak."

Just then, Javed and Liaqat arrived with their families. Javed froze seeing Khadija with Zafir. Liaqat asked quickly,

"What's going on? Why call us here—and with our families?"

"I didn't. Zafir did," Babar growled.

Zafir turned to them all,

"Not one of you ever asked Khadija how she was.

Not once."

"This is a family matter. You have no right to interfere," Javed snapped.

Zafir replied calmly,

"But in the case of my future wife… I do have a right."

Gasps followed. Bina jumped,

"Yes! Exactly!"

But Zafir clarified, pointing at Khadija,

"I meant her."

Chaos rippled through the room.

"M-Mama, did you hear that?! This witch ruined my engagement before it even began!" Bina cried.

Khadija was stunned. She tried to speak, but Zafir gently motioned for her to remain quiet.

"You just stay quiet," Babar snapped at his daughter.

Then to Zafir,

"Fine. If you want to marry her, take her and go. Do as you please. I'll speak to your father."

Zafir clapped his hands mockingly.

"You think I came for your permission?

You really think this is about marriage?

You should know by now… this visit is about something much bigger."

"Let's not do this in front of everyone—come inside, let's talk like adults," Babar pleaded.

"Yeah, why drag the family into this?" Javed echoed.

Zafir pulled out files and laid them on the table.

"This is Khadija's property. All the papers are here."

"P-property? What property?" Liaqat stammered.

"Over thirty crores' worth.

And you three stole it. You conspired and divided it among yourselves," Zafir stated.

The three brothers tried to laugh it off.

"Nonsense. He's lying. This boy is delusional."

"Get out of here!" Babar barked.

"Fine. I'll leave. And take these files to the police and social media.

They'll get the truth out of you." Zafir reached for the documents.

Panic set in.

"Wait! What do you want?" Javed finally said.

Everyone in the room froze. The truth now hung in the air.

"Just return what was stolen," Zafir said quietly.

"You're insane!" Liaqat shouted.

Zafir shot back,

"Yell all you want. I haven't even shared the cruellest truths yet.

Should I?"

"Stop! Just tell us what to do. We don't want a scene," Babar conceded.

"By tomorrow, the full amount should be deposited into Khadija's account."

After exchanging looks, Babar nodded,

"Fine. We'll do it."

But a new voice rose—firm and clear.

"I won't accept it."

It was Khadija.

Zafir looked at her, surprised. His eyes said: I asked you not to speak.

She turned to him.

"What you've done is another kindness I can never repay."

Then she faced her uncles.

"You hated my mother and me.

You disowned us. I never knew I had such wealth in my name...

And while you sold my father's property, I gave tuitions just to survive.

He never acknowledged me as a daughter—only as a disgrace.

So I reject every rupee tied to his name.

You can keep all of it.

I want none of it."

Then she turned softly to Zafir.

"I'm sorry. Could you drop me home?"

Zafir looked at her—worn, but still grounded.

"Come. Let's go."

And together, without another word, they walked out slowly... and left everything behind.

Scene 149

What Wasn't Hers, and What Is

They were driving back in silence—Zafir at the wheel, Khadija beside him. Neither said a word.

When they reached her home, Khadija looked over. His eyes stayed fixed on the windshield.

Softly, she asked,

"Are you upset with me?"

Still not looking at her, Zafir replied,

"No... but I am surprised. You dismissed everything I worked for—gave away what was rightfully yours to the people who wronged you."

Khadija didn't flinch.

"I'll explain that in a moment.

But first... why did you say all that about marriage back there?"

Zafir exhaled, glancing at her.

"I know how you feel about marriage and the very idea of a husband.

But I had to say it. Without that, they wouldn't have listened or returned anything to you."

Khadija studied his face, then said quietly,

"So you said it only to pressure them into doing the right thing."

Zafir nodded.

As she opened the door to step out, Khadija said,

"Then it's fine.

That property... it never belonged to me. The man who owned it never called me his daughter.

How could I claim anything in his name?

I'm sorry for what I did—please forgive me, if you can."

Zafir's voice was low.

"I'm not angry with you. So there's nothing to forgive."

As she stepped out of the car, Khadija paused and said in almost a whisper,

"What I left behind wasn't mine. So I left it behind, too.

What is mine... is still right here."

Then she turned and walked into her house, leaving Zafir in the car—eyes lowered, replaying that final line, unsure if he truly understood what she had just given him.

Scene 150

A Conversation Half-Finished

"Bhai jaan, I thought you'd tell me first if anything ever happened," Saira said softly over the phone.

Zafir hesitated,

"Oh come on, Gudiya... it's not what you think."

"It hurt me, you know—realizing you've started keeping things from me," she said, her voice low with disappointment.

"No, it's not that at all.

No matter what I feel or don't feel for her—she's someone who's been wronged.

I just wanted to help her get what she deserved.

But even after everything, she refused to take it," Zafir said, a touch of sadness in his tone.

"That part I understand. And honestly, I admire it," Saira replied.

"She seems like a girl with real self-respect.

But what hurts me is... why didn't you share your feelings for her with me?"

Zafir replied gently,

"Because I think this is one-way traffic."

"What do you mean? You think she doesn't care for you?" Saira asked.

Zafir's voice sank.

"She hates the words marriage and husband.

Affection or love? Those are miles beyond that, Gudiya."

After a pause, Saira said thoughtfully,

"Bhai jaan… will you give me Khadija's number?

I've asked before but you never shared it."

Zafir replied,

"I just don't want you bringing up anything about marriage."

Saira smiled through the phone.

"I won't say a word about marriage.

I just… want to talk to her."

Zafir dodged gently,

"Alright, let's talk about this some other time."

Scene 151

The Quiet Before the Ambush

"What do we do now?" Liaqat asked.

He was in a closed-door meeting with his two older brothers.

Babar clenched his fists in fury,

"That vile boy humiliated us—right in front of our own families."

Javed, frowning, said slowly,

"Bhai sahib, our real problem isn't Zafir. It's Khadija. Don't forget that."

"What do you mean?" Babar asked, narrowing his eyes.

Javed spoke with a note of anxiety,

"A month ago, when Zafir brought her here, she publicly refused the inheritance. But legally, that refusal means nothing.

If she files a case now—we'll all be behind bars."

Liaqat, cold and merciless, hissed,

"Letting her live was our biggest mistake.

If we'd crushed the serpent's head from the start, we wouldn't be here now.

It's not too late. Neither she nor Zafir have gone to the police."

Javed looked uneasy,

"But... what if they do after we move? What then?"

Babar leaned in, voice low and conspiratorial,

"Liaqat's plan might be our best option—and now is the time.

I've got word that Zafir's been missing from his apartment for almost a month.

I asked around. The unknown men keeping watch on him? Gone.

It looks like someone's already taken care of him.

I called Farooq in Canada—he claimed he didn't know anything, but his voice gave him away.

Something's happened—and he's hiding it."

Javed nodded grimly,

"Then this is our moment. But tell your man not to fail this time, Liaqat."

Liaqat, with a cruel smile, said,

"Don't worry. This time, he'll get it done.

We'll hear good news soon—and finally sleep with this sword no longer hanging over our heads."

Scene 152

The Alley and the Sirens

Khadija had just stepped out to buy groceries when a car blocked her path at the alley's corner.

Her heart skipped—these were the same men who had tried to abduct her once before.

Before she could even scream, a police jeep screeched into the alley like a windstorm. Officers jumped out, guns raised, surrounding the car.

Just then, a man in plain clothes appeared from nearby—he was the one who had alerted the police about the suspicious vehicle watching the neighbourhood. He was appointed by the FIA officer Jawad

Khadija stood frozen, stunned, as relief washed over her.

A police officer barked an order,

"Cuff them—and take them in. Treat them very well at the station. Leave nothing lacking. Let them enjoy our hospitality. "

Then he turned to her and said,

"Ma'am, please don't worry. We'll take care of these thugs—and the ones who sent them."

Khadija, still shaken, asked,

"Thank you... but who are they? They tried to kidnap and kill me once before."

The officer nodded.

"They're hired hitmen. The real criminals are someone else—we've been tracking them.

But you don't need to worry now.

You're safe. Just carry on with your day."

As Khadija turned slowly toward the grocery store, she couldn't help but reflect on how the police—so often feared and mistrusted—had been nothing like she'd expected.

For once, her fear had met its match... in justice that showed up on time.

Scene 153

The Bargain of Shame

"Why have we been brought here? We're respectable citizens of this country!" Babar protested angrily.

Javed leaned in,

"Bhai Sahib, call your lawyer. I'll ring up Farrukh. Once these officers get a call from above, they'll fall back in line."

Liaqat quickly dialled his bureaucrat friend.

The officer sitting across from them said nothing—didn't interrupt, didn't stop them.

When they were done making calls, he finally spoke:

"Done? Made all your calls? Now shut up and listen to me. If anyone interrupts me, I'll hang you upside down and beat you until all your so-called dignity drains out through your ears and nose."

The three men fell silent.

He calmly laid files in front of them.

"These contain every detail of your crimes, with proof—how you tricked your niece into signing power of attorney and legal papers, then left her abandoned in Turkey, and gobbled up all her property.

You've tried to have her killed multiple times.

And the hitmen you hired? They've turned state witnesses. We now have all the evidence we need."

Babar, now shaken, tried diplomacy.

“Is there… anything that can be done?”

The officer smiled coldly.

“Absolutely. When this case reaches court, you’ll return every penny you stole.

You’ll face public disgrace. And you’ll be handed life imprisonment with hard labour.

All of that can be done.”

Javed turned to Babar and Liaqat—they all understood the noose was now real.

“Is there another option? Something that could… make you happy?” he ventured.

“Instead of worrying about my happiness,” the officer replied,

“worry about your future.

There is an alternative.

In it, your public shaming can be minimized. Your sentence—reduced to three to five years.

Think about what you want to do.”

Babar swallowed hard.

“What’s this alternative?”

The officer slid a legal confession across the table.

“Sign this.

You’ll admit to defrauding your niece of her inheritance and agree to return it.

In court, your cooperation will earn you leniency.

You'll be sentenced in one or two sittings—and after three or four years… you walk free.

If not… you truly have no idea what's coming."

A month later, a magistrate court sentenced the three brothers to three years in prison, a fine of half a million rupees, and ordered the full restitution of Khadija's stolen property.

Khadija was summoned by the court. She appeared.

When she once again declined to accept the inheritance, the judge said,

"Legally, the amount will be deposited into your account.

What you choose to do afterward—keep it or donate it—is your call."

The very next day, Khadija walked quietly into a reputable trust—one run under the guidance of respected scholars—and donated the entire sum to charity.

Scene 154

The Answer That Hasn't Come

Six months had passed

Khadija had moved out from Aamna's mother's house and into a modest upper-floor portion rented from a friend of hers. One day, while tutoring children, her phone rang—it was Arifa.

Khadija turned to the children with a calm smile,

"Review your lesson. I'll be right back."

Then she picked up the phone.

"Ammi, why do you always call me just to say the same thing again and again?

My answer is still the same: I don't want to get married—not right now."

After listening for a moment, Khadija continued,

"Yes, I met with them like you insisted… but they were strange, Ammi.

The women looked at me like I was livestock on display—not a girl, but a goat for sacrifice."

Arifa said something else. Khadija's voice softened, but stayed firm.

"Ammi… I've let go of my stubbornness.

I no longer say I hate the idea of marriage or a husband.

But still—I'm not ready. Why do you keep pressuring me?"

When her mother asked something more, Khadija replied gently,

"Yes, I've started offering prayer.

I've stopped complaining. I've stopped demanding."

But when Arifa asked about him, Khadija's tone shifted—quiet and unbothered.

"I don't know where he is.

He hasn't contacted me even once in six months.

I've never called him either.

The few times you tried, his number was off.

What else can I say, Ammi… let's stop talking about him."

Her tone turned wistful.

"You mentioned coming to Pakistan for Eid. Will you visit me too?"

Then, with a trembling pause—

"But don't just leave from the gate like last time.

I really want to lay my head in your lap… close my eyes…

And forget everything in your arms."

After chatting a little longer, she ended the call, wiped away her quiet tears, and returned to teaching the children.

Scene 155

The Deflection of Shadows

A high-level meeting was underway in the underground bunker—its sole purpose: to present the final progress on the classified project.

SUPARCO's Chief Research Director addressed the room:

"For the past six months, this team has been confined within this bunker. Due to severe security concerns, none of you were allowed to contact the outside world or step out.

I truly regret the isolation—but it was necessary for your safety, and for the success of this mission.

Today, I am thrilled to announce that we've conducted the first successful trial of the device.

The results are promising.

We couldn't fully generate a spatial anomaly or a controlled wormhole—those remain beyond reach in our current environment.

But within our limited resources, we have achieved something extraordinary: a device that can manipulate the time-based quantum mechanics of surrounding airspace to create artificial deflection.

In simpler terms—

If an enemy fires a bomb or missile at us, we can now bend its trajectory away and intercept it with precision.

No country has this technology.

The next phase will involve transitioning this lab prototype into industrial production, which the Military Research & Development division will oversee.

Therefore, this research team is being dismantled starting today.

You're all free to return to your previous professions and to live like ordinary citizens once again.

And above all—you deserve congratulations. You've made history."

Zafir felt a rush of contentment—his idea had not only worked, it was poised to transform global defence. Packing up in his office, someone came in and said,

"Director would like to see you in his office."

When Zafir entered, the Director rose and embraced him.

"You are, without doubt, the hero of this project—the cornerstone.

Without you, none of this would've begun, let alone reached this milestone.

I didn't name you in the closing speech, and in the official papers, you're still listed as Scientist X. That was done purely for your safety.

The credit will go to a senior military officer—they face fewer risks and can appear as an institutional face to the world.

I hope you don't mind.

No one will ever know this was your creation.

But you are this nation's unsung hero—

And for that, I salute you.

We've arranged for your official employment at SUPARCO. You may begin after one week."

Zafir thanked him and stepped outside.

There was pride in his chest—not for fame, not for reward, but for the quiet truth:

He had built something impossible.

And now, for the first time in months... he would breathe the open air again.

Scene 156

The Number That Was Kept

Zafir had already informed his family that he wouldn't be in touch for six months. Now, stepping back into the world, he first called his mother and father. Hearing his voice, they were overjoyed. Then he spoke to his younger brothers as well.

He dialled Saira next, but she was out with her husband and daughter, so the call didn't go through.

Then, without hesitation, he drove straight to Khadija's last known address. But to his surprise, she no longer lived there. A different family had moved in—six months ago.

Zafir tried calling her number. It rang… and rang…

But she didn't pick up.

Worry crept in. Where is she? What if her uncles tried something again?

Anxious now, he called Arifa.

"Aunty, are you doing well? I was at a secure site for work over the last six months—no communication was allowed."

"I'm well, beta," Arifa replied warmly.

"I did try calling you a couple of times, but your phone was switched off. Are you okay? Did your work go well?"

"Alhamdulillah, yes. It went very well," he said with pride.

"Aunty… where's Khadija? Has she moved?"

"Yes, dear—she's relocated to another place. Did you need something from her?"

Zafir stammered slightly,

"N-no... not really. Just... asking.

Has she... changed her phone number too?"

Arifa smiled softly on the other end. She could sense it—something unspoken yet unmistakable. Both of them dancing around what they couldn't admit.

"Beta, I'll text you her new address.

She still has the old number too, though she doesn't use it. Not sure why she's kept it.

She's probably teaching right now—that's maybe why she didn't answer."

"Thank you, Aunty. Take care... we'll talk again soon."

And with that, Zafir ended the call—more certain of what he needed to do next... and less certain of what would be waiting on the other side.

Scene 157

One Call That Didn't Come, and One That Might

Before going to bed, Khadija—out of habit—pulled out her old phone and checked the screen. Her face lit up instantly.

The call.

The one she had waited for every single night these past six months.

Her heart pounded.

"He's back? But where was he? Should I call him now?" she whispered to herself.

She glanced at the time—11:30 p.m.

Her fingers hovered over the screen. Part of her burned to dial. But then she pulled back,

"He's probably asleep.

I'll call him in the morning."

Meanwhile, Zafir was pacing, waiting for that very call. But it didn't come.

He hadn't dared to call her on the new number.

Just then, Saira's call lit up his phone. Her voice, warm and cheerful, wrapped around him.

"Bhai jaan, it's been so long since I've seen you. Please come back now."

Zafir smiled,

"I miss all of you too. Especially your little doll, Safia.

She must think her uncle is the worst for not visiting yet."

Saira chuckled,

"Safia thinks her uncle Zafir is the best.

But yes—she is a little upset you haven't come to see her."

Their laughter danced through the line as she shared stories about herself and Safia. Then, sensing something unspoken, she asked:

"Bhai jaan... have you been trying to say something, and just couldn't?"

Zafir admitted softly,

"Yes, Gudiya. That's exactly it."

"But there's nothing between us you ever have to hesitate to say. What is it?"

Zafir took a breath,

"Can you... do something for me?"

"Of course. Just say it." She said.

He hesitated again.

"I'll text you a number. Can you..."

Saira smiled knowingly, finishing it for him,

"Yes, Bhai jaan. I'll call Khadija. I'll check how she's doing—and I'll tell you."

He blushed into the phone,

"Thank you. Please call her now. I'll wait for your call."

Saira smiled to herself,

"Yes, Bhai jaan. I'll talk to her now—and call you right after."

Scene 158

The Call That Changed Everything

Khadija was holding her old phone when her new phone rang. Startled, the old one slipped from her hand and landed softly on the carpet.

She picked up the call from the unfamiliar international number.

"Assalam-o-alaikum. Is this Khadija speaking?" came a cheerful, unfamiliar female voice.

Surprised, Khadija replied softly,

"Wa alaikum assalam... yes, I'm Khadija."

The voice brightened with warmth.

"So you're the Khadija I've been dying to speak to for ages—but bhai jaan never shared your number. I'm Saira."

Khadija blinked, startled.

"Z-Zafir's younger sister?"

"Yes, yes!" Saira laughed.

"How are you? You sound so lovely—I'm sure you must be just as beautiful."

Khadija smiled,

"I'm well, thank you. I haven't seen you, but Zafir once showed me a photo of your daughter—she's adorable, masha'Allah."

"Thank you! Bhai jaan had been working somewhere classified for the past six months—completely off the grid.

Maybe that's why you hadn't heard from him either.

He's back now—and he gave me your number, just to check on you... and to tell you he's doing well.

So, Khadija... what shall I tell him from your side?"

Khadija blushed.

"W-what do you mean?"

Saira teased gently,

"I mean... what message should I give bhai jaan from you?

But while you think about that, let me give you one from him."

"What is it?" Khadija asked, eyes wide.

Saira's voice softened playfully,

"I know every beat of my brother's heart. I'm his confidante and advisor.

There's something he might never say outright—

But he likes you.

A lot.

And he wants to marry you.

He never told me to say that—but I know.

And I'm asking you, from my own heart—

Please consider my brother. He'll cherish you. Truly.

So... what should I tell him?"

Khadija's face flushed with joy and shyness. She whispered,

"Tell him... to speak with my mother. Or... maybe your mother can."

Saira erupted with joy.

"Wow! You just fulfilled a wish we've all been silently hoping for!

From now on, I'll call you Khadija bhabhi, if you don't mind?"

"No... I don't," Khadija said shyly.

"Then I'm calling bhai jaan right now with this news.

Mummy, Daddy, both my younger brothers—we're all coming to Pakistan soon.

Because bhai jaan wants to settle there permanently.

And now I finally understand why!"

Saira laughed with a heart full of light.

Final Scene

Full Circle

Khadija looked at Zafir with a smile and asked,

“Why are we going to Turkey for our honeymoon?”

They were on a flight to Ankara. Zafir smiled back,

“There’s a reason, Khadija—you’ll find out soon.”

After landing, they took a taxi to their hotel. Khadija glanced around and said,

“Everything feels so beautiful now. And it’s all because of you.”

Zafir looked at her warmly,

“There’s something you said that I finally understood after we got married…”

“What was it?” she asked.

He replied,

“When I took you to your uncle’s house to reclaim your inheritance and you refused…

And later, when I dropped you off and you said, ‘Everything of mine is right here’—

You were talking about me, weren’t you?”

Khadija lowered her gaze, blushing.

“Back then, I used to rant about marriage and husbands.

When my heart and mind began to stir for you…

How could I have told you…?"

Words failed her. Zafir smiled,

"Looks like the hotel's here."

The next day, in another taxi, Khadija asked,

"Where are we going?"

Zafir gave her a knowing smile,

"To the very reason we came to Ankara for our honeymoon."

They got out near a quiet street and walked to a corner. Zafir gestured with a smile,

"Khadija, this is where we first met."

Khadija smiled,

"Where our heads bumped into each other."

Zafir grinned,

"So that our hearts could meet."

Khadija's eyes sparkled,

"I love you."

Zafir replied gently,

"I love you a million…"

Then he said,

"But now it's time for something very important.

The same thing we did here years ago out of desperation—

We'll do today for fun."

Khadija looked at him, confused,

“What thing, Zafir?”

With a wide smile, Zafir said,

“Khadija, let’s run.”

And with that, he darted off—

Khadija laughed and ran after him, joy rushing louder than the wind.

And so, what once began in shadows and survival, ended in sunlight and shared laughter.

THE END

Epilogue

Dignity is non-negotiable. Even when everything is stripped away—home, family, inheritance—your dignity is what you must never give up.

- Justice may be delayed, but not erased. The truth has its own timeline. What matters is not how soon it arrives, but how steadily you stand in its waiting.
- Love grounded in empathy doesn't seek to rescue—it chooses to stand beside. That's where trust is born, and where it endures.
- Family is not always defined by blood. Sometimes, your greatest allies come not from shared lineage, but from shared belief in your worth.
- Letting go can be an act of power. Refusing to accept ill-gotten wealth wasn't weakness—it was the boldest statement of self-worth.
- Don't mistake silence for weakness. Often, those who speak least have the strongest fire within.
- A husband and wife should resolve their differences, as unresolved conflicts can negatively affect their children's upbringing and emotional development.
- Recognizing brilliance is a virtue; channelling that brilliance toward meaningful, positive goals is an even greater one. True appreciation lies in harnessing talent with purpose, respect, and integrity.
- Seeking to amend one injustice by committing another only sustains the cycle of defiance. As portrayed in this novel, rebellion is not quelled by retribution, but embraced with empathy, trust, faith, and love."

Upcoming Novels by Aakh

Step into a world where the quiet strength of resilience, the weight of moral choice, and the silent currents of revolution intertwine. These forthcoming novels illuminate the human journey—not just in moments of love, triumph or tragedy, but in the nuanced spaces in between.

Beyond the inner landscapes of individual resilience, the author's forthcoming novels delve into the intricate web of relationships and the delicate tensions between tradition and modernity. Through vivid characters and immersive storytelling, these works navigate pressing social issues, celebrate the guiding light of religious practice, and examine the powerful influence of upbringing in shaping ethical, compassionate citizens. Woven into the narratives are echoes of political triumphs and moral reckonings—each story a tribute to the tireless pursuit of a more just, secure, and thriving society.

1. Panah (Refuge)
2. Baaghi (The Rebellion)
3. If & But : Logically Ever After
4. Romziana: Where the Wind Folds Light
5. A Whisper of Relief
6. Do or Die
7. Verbal Gymnastics
8. Nawab Sahib (Not-So-His-Highness)
9. Kind Strangers

10. Unfinished Dreams
11. Colourless Rainbow
12. Solace
13. The cursed one
14. Atonement
15. Mr. Ignoramus
16. Hero Zero
17. Benevolence
18. Hidden in Plain Light
19. One Life Isn't Enough
20. Retribution

Author's Bio

Writing under the pen name Aakh, the author is an electrical engineer by profession, working in the oil & gas sector. A Canadian citizen of Pakistani origin, he nurtured a lifelong love of writing that began as a quiet hobby—and has now found form in English through adaptations of his stories originally penned in Urdu. When not immersed in words, he finds joy in exploring new places and reading deeply.

Glossary of Urdu & Arabic Expressions

Abba - A respectful and affectionate word for "father" in Urdu.

Alhamdulillah - Arabic for "All praise is due to Allah"; often said to express gratitude or contentment.

Allah Hafiz - Urdu for "May Allah protect you"; commonly used to say goodbye with prayerful regard.

Amma - A respectful term for "mother" in Urdu.

Assalam-o-alaikum - Arabic greeting meaning "Peace be upon you."

Beti - Urdu for "daughter"; used warmly and respectfully.

Beta - Urdu for "son" or "child"; used as a term of endearment.

Bhai - Urdu for "brother"; also used to refer to male friends with familiarity and respect.

Chacha / Taya – Both mean "uncle," but chacha refers to the father's younger brother, taya to the elder.

Gudiya – A term of endearment meaning "doll," often used lovingly for a daughter or sister.

Insha'Allah - Arabic phrase meaning "If Allah wills"; used when referring to future hopes or plans.

Qibla - The direction Muslims face during prayer—towards the Kaaba in Makkah.

Qur’an - The holy book of Islam, revealed in Arabic to the Prophet Muhammad ﷺ over 23 years.

Sahib [Name] - A formal or respectful suffix in Urdu, akin to “Sir” or “Mr.” (e.g., “Jabbar Sahib”).

Sunnah - The traditions, practices, and sayings of the Prophet Muhammad ﷺ, serving as a moral and spiritual model.

Valima - The marriage banquet hosted by the groom’s family after the wedding—an Islamic tradition.

Wa Alaikum Assalam - The standard reply to “Assalam-o-alaikum,” meaning “And upon you be peace.”

Ya Allah - An emotional invocation meaning “Oh God!”—expresses plea, awe, or spiritual yearning.

www.ingramcontent.com/pod-product-compliance
Lightning Source LLC
LaVergne TN
LVHW052246200926
848481LV00002B/292